I0529761

THE FIREDANCE ANTHOLOGY

Words That Burn

Edited by Jae Erwin

Contributors

Gary Bonn

Janet Allison Brown

Louise Cole

Jae Erwin

Alison Gardiner

Stephen Godden

T. F. Grant

Alf Haywood

Shuna Meade

Lillian Reyes

Bill Sauer

Ren Warom

FIREDANCE BOOKS

Firedance: A Fairytale, Dancing Down From Heaven, Of All Things, To Kill a Wolf, Fire Starter, The Flame, From Seed, The Banyan Connection, Surreal, By the Throat, Firedance—The Ragged Dancers, Messing with Fire, On Tintock Tap, and *'Upa 'upa (The Firedance)* first published in the UK by Firedance Books in 2013.

Copyright © 2013: copyright is retained by the individual author of each piece of fiction contained within this anthology.

Cover and design copyright © Bill Sauer 2013

The right of the individual authors, whether identified by real name or pseudonym, to be identified as the authors of this work has been asserted in accordance with sections 77 and 78 of the Copyright, Designs and Patents Act 1988.

All characters in this publication are fictitious and any resemblance to real persons, living or dead, is purely coincidental.

All rights reserved.

This book is sold subject to the condition that it shall not be lent, resold, hired out or otherwise circulated. No part of this publication may be reproduced, stored in a retrieval system or transmitted, in any form or by any means, without the prior permission in writing of the authors, nor be otherwise circulated in any form of binding or cover other than that in which it is published and without a similar condition including this condition being imposed on the subsequent purchaser.

ISBN: 978-1-909256-22-4

Firedance Books

firedancebooks.com

CONTENTS

ABOUT THE FIREDANCE ANTHOLOGY: WORDS THAT BURN

IN WHAT SEEMS LIKE an age ago now, our authors started on a journey that began with the *Broken Worlds* anthology. Part way through writing and publishing it, one bright spark (no pun intended; well, perhaps a little one) suggested, "Hey, since we're doing this already, why don't we start a publishing co-operative?"

That prompted a search for a name — Firedance Books. Another bright spark (cough) proposed an anthology of stories on the theme of Firedance, assuming that such a strong visual would easily yield a wealth of stories.

It proved a great challenge and the result is a collection of stories, styles and genres to paint pictures in your mind, tug on your heartstrings and whisper in your ear.

Enjoy!

Firedance Books: Words That Burn

Jae Erwin,
Editor: *The Firedance Anthology: Words That Burn*

Firedance: A Fairytale

Janet Allison Brown

THERE WAS NO MISTAKE. Out there in the sea, far out, too far for safety, there was a child in the water. She or he — the distances were too great for clarity — appeared to be swimming towards the horizon along the great sparkling path laid down by the setting sun.

'It can't be,' she murmured, shading her eyes with one hand. With the other hand she stroked her chest with the habitual, soothing gesture of a mother to a fractious child.

There was a time, not so long ago, when Ellie had seen children everywhere. Now she wore her detached serenity like a steel girdle.

The child laughed — Ellie heard the sound tinkling on the breeze, and her heart gave a painful leap, despite the soothing hand.

Laughter?

Ellie moved gracefully outside onto the verandah, trying not to rush. But the sun, a perfectly round, orange ball just a moment ago, rested now on the rim of the world; a small arc of its circumference had sunk below the waves. As the sun set, her panic rose; she ran down the wooden steps onto the sand, hurried to the water's edge and, still shading her eyes against the glare, scanned the water, straining to hear what she thought she had — couldn't possibly have — heard.

There! That sound again! Laughter, high and tinkling, carrying over the waves.

'Come back!' cried Ellie in the cracked voice of a woman twice her age. 'You're too far out! Come back!'

The child laughed and turned. Ellie could just make out the pale moon of a girl's face. And then, without warning, the child rose up out of the water, turned to the horizon, and went dancing away on the waves along the flaming path of the setting sun.

'Come back!' screamed Ellie. 'It's getting dark! You're too far out!'

The sun was a semi-circle; it was a sliver; and the child was gone.

* * * *

Ted Baker had been here before; only the fine detail had changed. Once, Ellie had reported a child on a hilltop. Another time, she'd been convinced she heard a baby in the marina, and they'd had to search every boat. Every single boat. But there hadn't been an incident for over a year now. As local law enforcement, he had to take every case seriously but, well; he couldn't look Jim in the eye.

'So,' he said, aiming to sound business-like. 'The boats have been out for an hour now. There've been no sightings and no one's reported a missing child.'

Ellie stood wrapped in a blanket, glassy-eyed and still. She'd refused to move from the beach, despite her husband's best efforts. 'I saw her,' she said, without expression. 'There was a child in the water. No mistake.'

'In the water? I thought you said *on* the water.' Ted pushed back his cap and shifted from one foot to the other. He had calls to make and plans for the evening.

'Ted,' said Jim, putting his arm around his wife. 'Could you just take one more sweep of the bay?'

Officer Baker stood with his arms akimbo and jerked his head towards the water. 'Now you know there's no point. We won't see a thing out there in the dark.' He caught Jim's eye at last and changed his tone; he'd known Jim all his life. 'Don't worry, Ellie. Everyone sees things in the water sometimes, especially in bright, clear weather conditions like today's. It could have been a seagull, or a piece of plastic. Hell, it might have been a seal.'

He looked to Jim for confirmation. 'You've lived here as long as I have. You know the drill.' His voice faltered; he knew he was see-sawing between his two roles, personal and professional. He cleared his throat. 'When children go dancing out to sea, there are always frantic parents following hot on their heels. I get them waltzing into the office with all kinds of stories. But not this time.'

Dancing out to sea, waltzing into his office; that was a good one.

He'd have to write that one down. He'd like to have taken out his pad and pen right now, but it didn't seem appropriate.

He put a hand on Ellie's arm. 'Take it easy, old girl.'

She jerked away from his touch. 'Don't patronise me, Ted. I know what I saw.'

He gave up and retreated into his uniform. 'There's nothing to be done until daybreak. Jim. Ellie.' He walked away, murmuring, 'Danced out to sea, waltzed into my office, danced out to sea...' so that he wouldn't forget. One more phone call and he would go home to Sarah. Tuesday night was chicken night.

Damn; it was also maths homework night and Barney, his youngest, always struggled. Still, he could be at his desk by nine, which would give him three straight hours of writing. He'd have to be disciplined tonight and get to bed by midnight. If Ellie persisted with this fairytale of hers, he'd need to launch the boats again at daybreak.

He sighed. It was too bad for Jim. They'd all been jealous when he went away to university and brought home the cracker with the red hair. Lucky Jim; the woman was *gorgeous*. Even now, after fifteen years in the bay, they all stared when Ellie went by — men, women and children too. Hers was a regal beauty of Biblical proportions, and not the kind that faded with age either. If anything, age enhanced it; each year that passed laid a new depth on her.

Ah, but he'd take his homely Sarah any day of the week. Sarah *and the children*. He felt bad that he'd been sharp with them that morning. He was lucky to have children.

Damn, what was it again? Something about a waltz. Waltzing on the waves, was that it? Crap. He should have written it down, pretended to be writing case notes. Now he'd never remember.

He glanced back. He could just make out two dark, still figures on the beach, one frozen and fixed on the sea, the other leaning over her protectively, in defiance of whatever this night might bring.

Ted shivered and hurried home.

****

Ellie spent the night on the verandah, wandering down to the shore with a lantern every few minutes, then every half hour, then every hour, calling out, 'Are you there?'

'There's no one there,' said Jim. 'Come to bed, sweetheart. You were probably mistaken. And even if — hold it, I didn't say I didn't believe you. All I'm saying is that if you are right, Ted's right too: there's nothing we can do in the dark. Wait until morning.'

In the end he slept on the verandah too, on the hammock they strung up every spring and had to replace at each summer's end because the salt air ate away at the strings. He couldn't count the number of times in his life that he'd fallen through the bottom of a hammock. Ellie had fallen just once; after that, the hammock was replaced, like a seasonal marker, every year without fail.

He woke at a shout from the beach. 'She's there! Look, Jim!'

The sun was cresting the hills behind the house, promising another of those exceptionally clear, pure days; you could see for miles. Jim fell out of the hammock, picked himself up and stretched.

'Come on!' yelled his wife. 'Hurry up, lazy bones!'

She sounded happy; didn't she just say she'd seen the child again? Jim hurdled the verandah railings, landed heavily in the sand — damn, that used to be easy — and ran to his wife's side.

She stood barefoot, with her toes in the water, pointing out to sea. The sun behind them was kissing the water into a milky shade of aquamarine. Jim looked into Ellie's face; she glowed. He dutifully followed her outstretched arm and hand, looked out across the water and —

'Good God.'

At that moment, a path of light sprang to life between Ellie and the horizon. The sea shimmered with early morning haze except in the path cast by the sun; there it flashed a vivid gold and silver and orange. And clear as day, clear as that day's vaulted sky, a child swam in the new-born sunlight.

Jim stared. He stared and stared, and then he turned to his wife. 'She's still there?' he said incredulously. 'She's... what, she's been swimming *all night*?'

His wife shook her head and the sun tangled in her red hair, turning it, too, into flames. 'She's not still there, she's there *again*,' she said, laughing.

'She must be exhausted. She'll drown!' cried Jim. He turned and ran for the house.

'No, wait!' called his wife. 'Jim, it's okay. I think I understand now.'

But Jim would not be stopped. He phoned Ted and within twenty minutes the boats were re-launched and a helicopter, too, sent out from the nearby rescue centre. They spent the morning scouring the bay, and the two bays either side, and then further out into the open sea.

There was nothing to be found.

'Of course there wasn't,' said Ellie gently. It was her turn to put her arm around Jim, his turn to pace fretfully between shore and verandah.

'Damn it, I saw her, Ted,' he told his friend. 'Don't give me that about buoys and seagulls. I know what I saw, and it was a girl.'

'In the water or on the water?' said Ted drily.

Jim stopped his pacing. 'In the water, Ted. What do you think I am, a moron?' He glanced quickly at his wife; only yesterday evening she had told them the child stood on the water. But now she just laughed.

'We can't keep the boats out any longer,' said Ted. 'I'm sorry Jim. Call me when you've got something more solid.'

'And you call me when some frantic parents come waltzing into your office demanding to know why you didn't rescue their drowning child!' stormed Jim.

Waltzing — dancing — that was it! That great phrase from yesterday. Officer Baker took out his pen and notebook and hastily scribbled a note. 'That should do it,' he said.

'What are you smiling about?' demanded Jim. He looked at his wife. 'What are you both smiling about? Ellie, you were worried sick all night and now you're smiling?'

Ellie wrapped her arms around her husband's neck. 'It's okay, Jim. It's okay. Don't ask me how I know. I just know.'

He didn't go to work that day. In the afternoon he took a nap, and later Ellie persuaded him to barbecue. He felt in no mood for it, but it had been such a long time since she had asked him for anything — anything he could give her. They ate in the shade of the verandah; holiday-makers might forgo protection in pursuit of a tan, but when you lived here all year round you didn't mess with the UVs.

The sun hung low in the sky, preparing to set. Jim kept glancing at his wife, and she looked back at him serenely.

'Shall we?' she said at last.

He sighed. 'I don't know what you're playing at, Ellie.'

She gave him a look of breathtaking love and compassion. 'This isn't about me, darling. It's about all of us. Come with me. You'll see.'

She stood up and held out her hand. He hadn't seen her so *hopeful* in a long, long time. Not since; he winced. He could smell the clinic. He'd walked with her hand in hand, like this, down a corridor lined with notice boards covered in photographs of babies and toddlers, and cards.

Dear Dr Soud. Here is a picture of our lovely Emily, aged two months. We can't thank you enough... Dear Dr Soud. Heartfelt thanks to you and your team for our beloved twins, Amy and Joshua ... our delightful son ... our triplets! Thank you, thank you, for giving us our children. Without you and your team...

They had tripped down the corridor full of hope, and that hope carried them through the daily injections, the little room in which Jim had been required to perform his grim solo task, the harvesting of the eggs, the waiting...

IVF. Three little letters, thrown around like confetti. The first time he watched the enormous needle pierce his wife's ovaries to suck up the multitude of induced eggs — the first time, he'd thought he was watching a miracle. It got harder each time, as the scar tissue from the last attempt impeded this attempt's needle, so that it required force to puncture the ovaries and reach the eggs. Ellie, poor lamb, doped up but not unconscious, screaming at the pain she wouldn't remember afterwards.

IVF. The easy solution...

'Come on!' said Ellie, dragging him through the sand. 'Hurry!'

They reached the water's edge in time to watch the sea catch fire. They couldn't see her, at first, but they heard her: a silvery laugh, high and wild and beautiful.

And then they saw her, bobbing around in the water. She waved — did she wave? — yes, she was waving at them! Ellie waved back enthusiastically and Jim, in a daze, began to raise his arm.

'Look at that,' said a voice beside them. 'There's a girl in the water!' Barney Baker, Ted's ten-year-old, squinted into the sun. 'Dad told me about your girl. I thought I'd come out and take a look.'

Jim stared at Barney. 'You see her, right?'

Barney reluctantly tore his eyes away from the water and frowned at Jim. 'Of course, Jim. She's right there, in the water. What's she doing?'

'Dancing, of course,' gurgled Ellie, still waving. 'Hello sweetheart! Hello my darling! How are you?'

Did she know the child? Jim strained to see the face clearly, to make out identifying features. He couldn't, the distance was too great. And yet he had the strongest notion that he knew her...

'Look!' breathed Barney. The child, the girl, slowly rose up out of the water. She waved gaily at them, and then she stepped over the gentle waves, gingerly holding the hem of what might have been a little summer dress, as if to keep it dry. She turned away from them, laughing, and skipped and danced over the path of fire towards the setting sun.

'Good night sweetheart!' cried Ellie. 'God bless, my darling!'

It wasn't right. He should stop it, make it stop, do something. But what could he do? The sun had set, the sea was just the sea, darkening quickly in the fading light, and his wife stood beside him serene and lovely — and happy.

'What was that?' demanded Barney, shaking his head. 'What *was* that?'

'That,' said Ellie, 'was my daughter. That was our daughter, Jim.'

'We don't have a daughter,' he began, and stopped dead. He had recognised her.

****

In the two weeks of waiting, the time between inserting the dividing cells into Ellie and taking the pregnancy test, they had followed Dr Soud's advice.

'Act pregnant,' he'd said. 'Believe you're pregnant. Do the things pregnant couples do.'

'Will it help?' Ellie had asked hopefully, ready to believe anything.

'It won't hurt,' he'd said, looking at Jim.

Jim understood. Act pregnant, because then, if it fails, at least you will have had the experience of being pregnant. It will be one less thing denied to you, one small thing to cling to for the rest of your life. Once, I was pregnant; there was life inside me, for a moment.

So they'd pretended. They'd acted pregnant and then, when it failed, it killed them. It made it ten times worse because, each time, a child had died — not some cells that failed to divide, not an idea, but a child, fully conceived in their imagination.

This child, this fire-dancing girl in the sea, was one of their imaginings. She was their daughter.

****

Ellie lay fast asleep in the hammock, a little smile on her face. From time to time she muttered something, but these were peaceful, contented sounds, not the pain-filled cries of earlier times, the times before the girl in the sea.

Jim sat awake staring out at the dark waves. The moon was tiny, a small sickle in the sky, but the stars were voluminous, swirling like a Van Gogh canvas come to life.

No; wrong way round. The sky didn't represent the picture; the picture represented the sky. Jim wondered why art so often informed his response to nature, and found the answer right there in front of his eyes: because the sky was too vast and the ocean too deep. Nature needed to be tamed, on a canvas or a page or a screen, or no one was really *safe*...

He heard footfalls across the sand. For a moment he froze, genuinely afraid at what might be coming at him from out of the sea; and then he jumped a mile as Ted Baker's ample figure and gentle, deep voice came out of the soft night.

'You awake, Jim?'

'Jesus, Ted. I am now.'

Ted chuckled. 'I didn't mean to startle you. Thought you'd see me a mile off, what with this starlight and your extrasensory perception.'

'Very funny. What's on your mind?'

Ted sat down heavily beside him. 'What do you think?'

Jim nodded. 'Barney told you, huh?'

'He was surprisingly calm about it. Told me he'd seen your daughter dancing on the water.'

'On the water or in the water?' asked Jim, and Ted gave a gentle laugh.

'Well,' said Ted. 'Are you going to tell me about it?'

'How's your book coming along?'

'All right, I suppose. It's a long time coming, but it's coming. Some days it just flows right out of my pen. Other days, it's like pissing kidney stones.'

Jim took his turn to chuckle. 'When are you planning to finish?'

'It'll take as long as it takes.'

'Sarah's a patient woman.'

'Yes she is and you're changing the subject.'

'Yes I am,' said Jim. He nodded towards the gently snoring form of his wife, and the two men got up off the verandah steps and began to walk along the beach.

'I don't know what to tell you, Ted. There's a child in the water, at sunrise and sunset, and she's my daughter.'

'You mean like a fantasy thing. A shared fantasy between you and Ellie, the daughter you always wanted.'

'Is that what Barney said?' demanded Jim.

Ted sighed. 'No. He said she was real all right. He just about scared his little sisters half to death. Something about her rising up out of the water and dancing towards the sun.'

Jim raised his eyebrows and nodded slowly. 'That's about the long and short of it.'

Ted stopped in his tracks. 'Really, Jim? Is that really how it was? Because if you ask me, what we're looking at here is hysteria, a sort of auto-suggestion thing.'

'Barney — '

'Barney's a child and like all children he's suggestible. Now don't get all upset. I don't think you're lying or anything. I just — well, listen to yourself, Jim.'

'Come at daybreak,' said Jim. 'I don't know what to tell you. Just come at sunrise, and see for yourself.'

****

Jim came at sunrise, and he brought Sarah with him. Sarah said that if Jim and Ellie were misguided or, worse still, if they were being haunted, then it was her and Ted's business, as their closest friends, to be misguided or haunted right alongside them.

She meant it, too. Alone among their friends, Sarah understood the never-closing wound, the humiliation and grief that Ellie suffered every day. As she often told Ted, you could have all the emancipation you liked: female behaviour was as old as the hills and not about to change any time soon. When grown women got together they talked about kids. Schooling them, raising them, cuffing them; having them too young or too late or just plain having them. Children were the tomorrow that justified today.

And Ellie had to stand by and listen, hunting the moment to contribute some small comment to hide the fact that she would not be accompanying them into the future, her story lay in the past.

So Sarah came too, to stand beside her friend while her friend looked across the sea to watch her never-born daughter dance in the sunlight. That's what friends were for. 'And if you ever put this in one of your stories,' Sarah told her husband, 'I will divorce you and take the children with me.'

They arrived with minutes to spare. Ellie and Jim were already standing on the shore. 'We brought Barney along,' said Sarah, squeezing her friend's arm. 'He wanted to see the child again.'

Ellie smiled at her, and Sarah drew an astonished breath. She'd grown used to Ellie's beauty, as used to it as one ever could be. But this was something new. Ellie was vital, more physically present than ever before. The grace and serenity were no longer otherworldly; they were entirely human.

They lined up on the shore, Ted and Jim, Sarah, Ellie and Barney, and waited. The darkness intensified; the stars faded and all was silence and anticipation. And then a milky blue invaded the black, grew paler, lighter, a piercing line of light appeared on the hills behind them, like a shot of metallic thread through a navy scarf, and suddenly it seemed as if the whole of creation shouted out at once. All of them, afterwards, swore that they heard something loud and joyful.

After that it all moved quickly: the sun crested, laid out a path between the little group on the beach and the horizon, and then set fire to the waves.

'There she is,' said Ellie in a whisper, taking a little dancing step on the sand. 'Good morning, beloved.'

'Dear God,' breathed Sarah.

The child raised an arm, waved to them. And then there were two children. There was no mistake. Two children rose out of the water and stood, half-way between the shore and the horizon, looking back at the beach, squinting into the sun, laughing.

'Johnny?' said Ted, and he sank to his knees in the sand. Tears streamed down his face. 'Johnny!' he cried, reaching out towards the dancing figures.

'Who?' said Barney.

Sarah pulled him towards her, put her arms around him. 'Our first child,' she said, resting her lips on Barney's head, but still gazing out to sea; she would save her tears for later, when they wouldn't disturb the view. 'You would have had an older brother, but I miscarried. We named him anyway. Johnny.'

****

The clear days were over. The clouds gathered all afternoon, and although the small, hopeful party huddled along the shore that evening, the rain pocked the sand around them and watered the sea. No path of fire, no discernible sunset.

It might have been the light. It might have been the clarity. It wasn't plastic, or buoys, or even seals. First there had been one child, then two, and then a dozen or more. They rose up out of the sea and they danced along the flaming path of the sun to the horizon. But first they waved at the spectators on the shore; and always they laughed.

'I don't understand,' said Ted roughly. 'Why would God let those kids live in the sea like that? All alone.' There had been soft bedding in a cot for Johnny, and a room with fluffy clouds painted on the ceiling. Instead, Johnny danced on watery flames forever. And not just Johnny. 'I don't know how Ellie and Jim can stand it.' Ted shook his head and turned his face away from Sarah.

'That's because you're thinking about it all wrong.' Sarah dropped her hand on his shoulder. 'The children were happy, Ted. We didn't give them flesh to wear or a life to live but they were happy. They were safe. I don't have to worry about Johnny any more. Ellie can sleep nights knowing her girl isn't lost in some dark forever because her mother never came for her.'

'You know that makes no sense,' said Ted, fumbling for his wife's hand.

Across town, in their house on the beach, Ellie and Jim sat whispering and giggling like children, making plans for the future.

Dancing Down From Heaven

Ren Warom

THE FALLING STAR CAME as a thin streak of blazing yellow against the pale grey patina of the afternoon sky and, for Marget of the Spring, it ended up being rather a personal experience. Its impact created a mighty explosion in her yard, the burst of blinding light and sound forcing her Genderel chicks underground for a full week and stopping the Barm from milking.

After hiding behind the back door for fully twenty minutes grasping a broom, cursing her widowhood for forcing her to face this trial alone, and whispering tight-worded prayers to the Meadow God Yaw and the Spring King Haseb, Marget finally found the courage to open the door. And what a sight awaited her.

'Oh Haseb's knob, look what it's gone and done to my Genderel yard!'

Where the yard once was, only a tangle of Willfletch switches used to weave the fence and torn boughs from the Yarrow tree planted for shade remained.

'That's a muddle and no mistake. Oh well, it won't clear itself.'

Broom abandoned to the floor, Marget bustled out the door, rolling up her sleeves over sun-browned, beefy forearms that in her youth made her ashamed and now pleased her immensely with their strength and practicality. As she reached the wreck of her yard, she leaned in to start untangling the mess when it moaned, quite loudly, else she'd not have heard it over the ringing in her ears.

Marget shrieked and leapt back a good five feet. 'God help us, there's a monster in there.'

The moan came again. It was terrible loud, but didn't sound monstrous at all on second hearing, only profound and deep and agonised, rather like her late husband Beng's moaning that time the Physic had to come round to set his busted leg. Marget bit her lip, gathered her nerve, and approached the tangle.

'Hello?' she called tentatively. 'Are you hurt?'

The moan came again. Definitely not a monster, surely some poor bugger in there bleeding half to death all over the Genderel burrows.

'Well,' she said to herself briskly, and not without a good helping of irritation, 'we can't be having that.'

Not a woman to waste ready-rolled sleeves, nor shy from a touch of hard labour, Marget waded on in to the thicket and began to unweave the mess. As the sun rose to the centre of the sky Marget, wringing with sweat and fed up from having to give constant reassurance to the moaning whoever in the muddle, finally broke through to the poor bugger, and stopped dead, arms elbow-deep in scratchy Willfletch, scream frozen within her freckled chest.

Dangling in a thick tangle of Willfletch and Yarrow was the most extraordinary creature. In the main it looked much like the Frome, her people, but differed in too many ways for her to ever call it Fromian. Its skin, rather than solid, sun-weathered brown, was black as char, smoked much the same, little curls wisping off like phantom fireflies, dancing across that black surface as though to some music Marget couldn't hear. And the creature was hairless. Not a Frome in all the Gedland without a good head of hair and, if male, a chest-deep beard to boot more often than not.

But it was the eyes marked the most of the difference, the eyes that caged the scream within her chest. Black as coals, they were, and smouldering with lightning lines of red, demonic to behold, but filled with such pain, such misery, that she could scarce bear to look. The eyes of a fallen angel those and, wrapped in a broken mess about the branches it hung from, the wings to match, made of a hard substance sharp as Wartle spines, stretched with silken stuff that shimmered like sunlight on water.

Marget hissed to herself, made the sign of warding. 'What in all the bells are you?' she said to the creature, then shrieked outright when it replied in her own tongue, in a voice of crackling flames over green Yarrow:

'Hizak. My name is Hizak.'

Through the slight dulling and ringing of her ears from the immense explosion, his voice sounded fearsome and alien as his appearance, but those eyes, the sadness, the hurt in them, held Marget suspended from unreasonable terror and she slowly calmed, though her hands clutched at the sweat-drenched fabric over her bosom. She gave him an accusing glare, angry at her own fears, angry at the mess he'd made of her Genderel yard, furious at having wasted half a day only to suffer this unnatural encounter.

'How are you here in my Genderel yard, angel?'

'I fell.'

'That much is obvious,' Marget scoffed, brusque, it not being in her nature to miss what sat right before her eyes. 'I mean, how is it you fell? Was heaven not enough for you?'

The creature Hizak appeared amused by this, despite his obvious pain. 'I am not fallen from heaven. There is no heaven beyond your sky, only the deep well of the void and such an abundance of life it beggars comprehension.'

Marget blinked, her fury quite deflated. Being a pragmatic woman, this refutation of her beliefs did not shake or astound her, it only made her more annoyed. What was this creature? She unlatched her fingers and crossed her arms, putting on her face the disapproving glare Beng once earned for not bringing in enough firewood of a cold evening, or failing to earn sufficient funds, thereby forcing Marget to barter.

'Oh. Well then, Hizak of the Well,' she said sternly. 'If there's no heaven up there, where did you fall from? You tell me that.'

'The sun,' he said to her, 'I fell from the sun.' And the sadness in his eyes leaked into his voice and filled the air around her with melancholy heat like late midsummer when the cool of autumn approaches and the heavy weight of fruit begins to rot upon the bough.

'Of all the absurd...' Marget contained herself as Hizak groaned again, a sound of infinite distress. Whatever manner of creature Hizak was, whether he spoke the truth or not, he was in pain and in need of help. Not only that, but she could see now that he *was* bleeding, though it looked nothing like blood, and that substance dripped directly into the Genderel burrows. 'If I want to eat any eggs within the next moon cycle I need to get you off these branches,' she said, brisk and determined.

She looked him in those dark, unnatural eyes. 'I'm going to get your wings as untangled as I can, but then I'll just have to haul you off. Are you able to help?'

Hizak nodded. 'I am.'

'Good.'

Marget stepped forward, wary, and, under Hizak's crackling gaze, set to gentle extraction of the many branches from about the curious matter of his wings. Though she tried at first not to touch them, eventually necessity forced her to handle them directly, and it was then she faltered. The shimmering stuff enchanted her. It was nothing like flesh, though warm to the touch, and of a toughness that astonished her, for not one branch had managed to pierce it, nor break the spines it stretched between.

'I'll give you this, Hizak angel,' she said, as she reluctantly continued her work, 'your wings are nowhere near as easily damaged as your flesh. A good thing, too. I'll wager even the Livestock Physic's not seen aught like this in all his days.'

'That is because they are not flesh.'

Marget tugged one wing fully free. 'Nonsense,' she snapped, 'this comes direct from your back, I see it with my own eyes.'

'It is attached to me, attached within me. I was designed to have them attached at birth, and so they were, but I was not born with them.'

'How were you born then, and who attached them?' she asked, too curious to hold her tongue.

'I was born, as we all were, in the great machine, and it was the machine gave me my wings.'

'No mother?' she asked, her heart aching for him all unbidden. 'No father?'

'I had no need of either,' he said to her, with such simple acceptance of the fact it soothed her hurt for him. 'The machine was both mother and father to me, I knew no sorrow.'

Marget stroked the material — for it must be material if not flesh — with a wondering hand. 'What is this stuff, then, if not flesh? I've never seen the like.'

Hizak frowned. 'Not even in the Metros?'

Marget stepped back, tilting her head and eyeing him with sudden suspicion. 'The Metros, you say?'

'The places filled with folk like yourself, and many machines that work without assistance.'

'I know what they are,' she said, dismissive, getting to work on his other wing. 'There's ruins of one not far from here that Beng, my late husband, was always nagging at me to go see. But I've no interest in what's past. Too concerned with surviving day to day in the here and now.' Marget moved to take his arm and paused, uncertain, her eyes upon the small curls of smoke dancing from shoulder to fingertip. 'Will your skin burn me?'

'Burn you?' Hizak shook his head. He appeared distracted, distressed in some way that might or might not have been his current pain. 'No. I control the temperature. I will not let you come to harm.'

Marget breathed deep and reached for Hizak's arm, sighing relief as, good as his word, it did not harm her. She slung that limb across her broad shoulders and said, 'Give me all the help you can, you're a big'un and no mistake, big as my middle lad, Jorg.'

Hizak's large hand curled about her shoulder showed his understanding and Marget braced her back, her feet, and heaved. With much tearing of branches and a low shout of pain from poor Hizak, he was finally loose.

'Thank you...' He faltered and said apologetically, 'I'm afraid I do not know your name.'

'Marget. Marget of the Spring.' Nodding a belated greeting, Marget pulled up a large Yarrow bough she'd put to one side close by, and gave it to him to use as support.

'Thank you, Marget of the Spring,' he said to her formally, and slowly they made their way across the yard to the house, where she settled him on a simple, scratchy sofa.

He laid there, a smoking coal, watching her as she patched up his many wounds. When she was finished, he spoke again, his wood-smoke-and-fire voice rippling with unease.

'Please, tell me about the ruined Metros. Is it the only ruin?'

Marget sat back on her heels. 'Only one I know of, and it might be a ruin but none of them machines have stopped moving in there yet, far as I know.'

'But it is unoccupied?'

'Of course.'

'Are the other Metros in ruins?'

'No. Only Pellor, and that was a matter of bad luck, or perhaps good. It all depends on what you see as luck, don't it?'

Hizak leaned toward her, his obsidian eyes sparking red fires of hope. 'So the other Metros are occupied?'

A crack of disbelieving laughter broke from Marget's mouth. 'There's not been an occupied Metros for over a hundred years. Last was Ingelsy, over in the Holvstead. It carried on for perhaps six years after all the others were deserted, but now it's the same as the rest, just empty streets and buildings full of machines as never stop moving, never stop working. A meteorite shower hit Pellor, the ruin near here, but, like I said, it still just keeps on working, though it's all but tore apart and blackened to cinder by fires. It's why I didn't want to go with Beng, if I'm honest. Something plain disturbing about that place, those machines haunting it like ghosts.' She sighed. 'My Beng was fascinated by them, though they shook him up something proper the one time he went to look. Morbid, that's what.'

For a moment, Hizak appeared unable to speak. The smoke on his skin rose in dense clouds until some of the fibres of her sofa began to fizzle. It was at this point Hizak found a measure of control, his skin smoke slowly receding back to dancing curls, and then he found his voice; it came out of him wreathed in sheer desperation. 'Please. I must see it. I must see with my own eyes.'

Marget stared at him. 'I wouldn't even go with my Beng. Why would I go with you?'

'Please.' Hizak's face was desolate, broken. 'I beg of you. I must see Pellor.'

'You sent my Genderels underground, destroyed my yard and my Yarrow, lost me a full day of work that'll cost me crops, and now you want me to take you to that place? Did you strike your head as you fell?'

Hizak grasped her hands in his and said desperately, 'I will help you restore your yard, fetch out your Genderel, gather your crops, upon my honour. I owe you a debt and will repay it. But I *must* see Pellor, it is vital.'

Having worked alone the thirty years since Beng's death, breaking her back to survive, to raise her sons and send them into apprenticeships so they would not be forced to face the never-ending hand to mouth struggle against the land, the offer of help came as an alien but strangely comforting notion. So much so that Marget found herself seriously contemplating taking this poor creature to Pellor, a place she'd sworn to never see because there were some things that were unnatural and that was that.

As she thought, and considered, she came to realise that Hizak was as strange a thing as Pellor itself. Yet here she was, tending him on her sofa like he was one of her own sons, warmed not only by the gentle radiation of heat from his smoking skin, but by his offer of labour. In light of that, why was she so set against seeing Pellor? Perhaps in truth it would end up being no more distressing than this encounter. The idea settled her mind and she made her decision.

'Fine then. I'll take you to Pellor, but you be good as your word, you help me here on my farm. For a whole cycle of the moon and no less, mind.'

The relief on Hizak's face made her feel as though she'd reached out and lifted from him an unbearable burden. 'I promise,' he said.

'Then we'll go. We'll go in the morning. Sooner we get it over and done, sooner I can restore my yard and fetch in my crops.'

****

As first light crept over the far hills, Marget stood in her courtyard, harnessing her ageing Felding to the cart. Halfway through the complicated task of strapping on the bridle, Hizak hobbled out of the back door, leaning heavily on his Yarrow bough and blinking with sleepy eyes into the dawn glare. His skin seethed in the growing sunlight, as though it were drawing the warmth into itself.

'Do you need any help?' he asked, though his many wounds made it impossible for him to move with much ease.

Marget paused, surprised. 'No, thank you. Did you eat the gruel I left?'

Hizak smiled, white teeth flashing in smoking black flesh. 'I did, it was delicious. I think I will enjoy eating, at least, whilst I am here.'

Done with the straps, Marget turned a curious gaze upon her patient. 'Are you missing your home? Is it painful to be here?'

Hizak paused to consider. 'No. It is simply... different. I have yet to decide whether such difference is painful or not, and pain is a luxury I can ill afford.'

Marget's smile was grim; she understood that sentiment only too well. 'Come on, let's get you settled in the back, it's a good three hours at a stout trot to Pellor.'

The journey was silent, although none of it uncomfortable, Marget having never developed the taste for small talk and Hizak requiring all his energy to cope with the pain caused by the bumping of the cart on the ill-kept stone roads. When they were nearing Pellor, Hizak spoke and, from the shock in his voice, it was clear their journey had impacted him hard.

'Are there no large towns, no cities at all?'

Marget shrugged. It was no shock to her; this was her home, nothing unusual in it. 'Not so as I'd be aware. There's none right up to the coast both sides of Frome at the very least. When folk left the Metros, it was just a thing as happened. Natural like.'

'You are all crofters?'

'Crofters, crafters, weavers, bakers, steelmen and more. Everything that's needful. Even got ourselves a few storytellers and music players, though they don't do it as a living, we're not frivolous like that. Not one thing to be done as doesn't involve an early rise, a late to bed and hours of hard work between the two, especially crofting.' Marget pursed her lips, a look of determination. 'I didn't want crofting for my boys. Weather goes bad, that's your food gone to rot.'

'A hard life, then?'

'It's hard to make a living in any craft, but what's worth having as takes no grafting?'

'Nothing much,' said Hizak. 'Nothing much at all.'

'You work hard, then, up on the sun?' Marget was more than a little intrigued, though full of deep unease, about his solar origination. The thought that beings such as he lived upon the sun had her awed and terrified as if she were a child again, sat on her Great-Grandmarn's knee, hearing tales of the cities and their ever-moving machines.

'We do not ever stop working,' Hizak said simply, 'because the sun does not cease to shine for us.'

His words struck Marget hard. 'Grief,' she said, 'and there I thought crofting was a trying life.'

'It wasn't trying at all.' Hizak's reply was so soft, Marget, what with her hearing still affected from the previous day's explosion, didn't catch his words.

'Eh?'

Hizak smiled and repeated himself, loudly this time. 'It wasn't trying.'

Marget shot him a wide-eyed glance. 'Why ever not?'

'Because,' he replied, 'we were dancing.'

****

Pellor rose into view like a wound across the horizon, a gunmetal penumbra of broken spinets and charred rubble, rising out of the earth like some cursed forest in a folk tale, full of danger and uneasy spirits. Marget halted the cart at the outskirts and, with great reluctance, aided Hizak out of the back.

'You sure you have to go in?'

Hizak nodded. 'I'm sorry, but I must see. I must see a machine.'

Marget pressed her lips together. 'Then let's be doing it, before I lose the will.'

With her support and the aid of his Yarrow bough, Hizak walked with her into the Metros proper, through avenues crammed with fallen stone and warped metals, eerie in their abandonment. The sound of machines in the distance filled the air with metallic whispers, and a wind blew that made Marget shiver, even though the sun shone bright.

They travelled a good distance into that forest of metals and crumbled stone, until they happened upon one of the ever-moving machines. A blackened thing of melted char it was, a stumbling spectacle of multiple limbs, like a silver centipod, blind and aimless. Marget wanted to scream at the sight of it but, much like Hizak's sadness in the wreckage of her yard, a hollow desperation in its movement stilled the fear within her. How could she be afraid of such a pathetic thing?

'Poor thing,' she found herself saying instead, watching it struggle over jagged spikes of metal and falls of rock. It sensed them. She could tell by the way it lurched in their direction then stalled, as though uncertain of its own senses. The action sent a shiver of sadness through her bones. How terrible to be so useless and yet so desperate for a use. 'It doesn't have anything left to do, but it can't rest,' she said, 'even though it's all but burned to a cinder.'

When she received no response, Marget looked up at Hizak. He stood leaning onto Yarrow bough and Marget's shoulder as if only those two things were holding him upright. His face shone pure misery, dejection, as though more were lost than this vast place, as if part of his own self had died with it.

'They are all this empty,' he said.

She answered, even though it was not a question. 'All as empty as this. These places are not homes, they're reminders of a lost past, one we don't want back.'

'Tell me why.'

'Why it happened? Why we left?'

He nodded, tried to speak, but no words left him, only a small, choked noise filled with too much despair, and Marget said, 'It started here, after the shower. In truth I know only the history as it was told me on my Great-Grandmarn's knee.'

'Tell me,' Hizak pleaded.

'Well. All right.' She settled Hizak down on a stand of rock that might once have been the bedrock of a great building, sat next to him and began, uncertain at first, then with greater confidence as tales she'd not thought about since childhood slowly returned to her. 'Before the meteorite shower, we all of us lived in the Metros. We were tended by the machines, never doing nothing for ourselves and grown lazy, or so my Great-Grandmarn put it, and she should've known, she lived in a Metros as a child, left with her Marn and Pop when she were nearing her ninth summer. She said we didn't question how things got to be that way, just like I don't much wonder on the way my life turned out, I just get along with living it. But then everything changed when the shower hit.' Marget lifted a hand to encompass the view. 'You see for your own eyes the damage done to Pellor. Well, that wasn't the reason. Though it were bad, they could've stayed on, fixed the damage.'

'What caused the desertion, then?'

'The machines themselves,' Marget told him. 'Great-Grandmarn said we'd assumed they were worked by others, by people like us, people we didn't know, with lives like our own, simple and soft. But people died in vast numbers during the shower, and after it, and the machines just carried on working. It became clear to folk that they were moving all on their own, and at last we began to wonder about something. We began to wonder about the machines. Who was working them, what were they doing here? Course, because no one knew the answers, we got to being scared of them. Fear got so bad folk stopped wanting the machines around them, started to avoid them. But there weren't no place to hide from machines in the Metros. Great-Grandmarn said the machines kept trying to do things for people, so folk just up and started to leave, to get away from them. Couldn't go to other Metros, they were full, and there were machines in all of them, so they went out to the unbuilt spaces between. Once those left behind realised the machines wouldn't follow them as left, they all started leaving too. First from the ruins of Pellor then, as word spread about the machines, all the rest one by one, until the Metros were emptied.'

'But, how did they survive without the machines, those first deserters?'

'That's it, isn't it, why we're all small crofters and little hamlets, because most didn't. Those that did, those that survived, learned to work the land, to work wood and steel, to raise cattle. I'm kin from those folk,' Marget said proudly. 'Born of the survivors. I live the life they built, just like those in the Metros lived the life was built for them till they realised it weren't no life at all.' Marget spat with obvious disgust on the rubble at her feet. 'And so it weren't. Who wants to be waited on hand and foot, to be soft and helpless? Beggars belief.'

Hizak's eyes had thus far been wandering the ruined Metros, watching the last machines, crippled remnants, crawl the wreckage, sensing that there were beings sat right in their midst yet unable to find them, therefore unable to reach them, but now, he turned those simmering coals to Marget and said, 'Your life is such a struggle. You must do everything or you do not eat, you do not survive. Do you think that it is a better life than what was had here? Truly?'

Marget didn't need to think on it. Despite the hardship, the gruelling hours of labour, her fight to give her sons a different, less uncertain life, Marget knew where she belonged, knew what gave her satisfaction. 'I go out in the morning and hear my Genderels sing,' she told him. 'I watch the sunrise, the Robfoots and Sporrins diving through the clouds. That solid sun-up to down of labour ahead of me matters not a whit, even the seasons I get no crops. There's always a way to survive, if you know how, and I was raised knowing how. Raised my boys knowing, too, though they've gone to other crafts. Everything we possess is the work of our own two hands.' She nodded and offered him a smile. 'There's a lot there to make a body satisfied, right enough.'

Hizak regarded her with a sober gaze, his sadness filling the air between them. 'You think the people who lived here were less, don't you?'

Marget inclined her head. 'I do. They lived the life of babes in arms. Nothing to be proud of in having everything done for you when you're fit to do it yourself, having these machines nursemaid your every waking second. That's no life. We're well rid of these places, this life. There's not a soul amongst my people, not even the young, would come back. There's folk who like to visit and watch the machines, folk even more fascinated than my Beng, but it's only a hobby.' She shuddered, and said, 'If you can call a thing like that a hobby.'

Hizak smiled at her, then his gaze drifted back to the machines in the ruins. 'The machines, they are our doing.' He spoke in the manner of a confession, his shoulders low, his skin crackling as though on fire.

'What?'

'My kind, the Fire Dancers, *we* make the machines work. We harvest the sun for energy and fill great engines, which power the machines from afar. It is why they cannot leave the city; it is their source of power, power that we send down to them, that is being sent down even now. Though I am gone, the remainder of my kin will continue, unceasing, until the last of them falls.'

'Are there many of you?'

Hizak's reply was distant, thoughtful, unutterably sad. 'There has not been a new Fire Dancer born in decades. The machine that made us stopped working. Perhaps you could say that it died, in as much as a machine can die. I am one of the last of my people; there are only thirty in all remaining. Now only twenty-nine will dance.' He swallowed and said, his voice shaking with misery, 'And it appears that my journey here was for nothing.'

Marget laid a hand upon his arm, unconcerned about whether it might burn her in his current state. 'You fell on purpose?'

He nodded. 'We waited for someone to fix the machine, but it remained broken. We decided that one of us had to come, to make them fix our machine, or all of us would perish, both above and below.' He smiled down at her, infinite sadness in it. 'But the Metros are long gone. The world we worked for has passed beneath us whilst we were dancing.'

Marget's heart squeezed soft sympathy. Despite his appearance, Hizak had nothing of badness in him. He was a good soul and she did not like to see him brought so low. 'You weren't to know,' she said. 'It's not your fault the machines were making babes of us all. We were told folk such as us in the long ago created the machines, the Metros. Reckon the same folk made you, too. So who's to blame? You for doing what you were made for, or them that made you?' Her hand tightened on his arm. 'Will you go back, tell the others to stop, let the machines go still? Can you?'

Hizak looked up to the sun, he spread the shining gloss of his wings out behind him and Marget, the breeze they made caressing her skin soft as feathers. 'These solar wings of mine are not strong enough to get me through the earth's outer shell of gases once more. This journey was to be my last. I made it in the belief I could bring hope to my people and to yours.'

'So you're stuck here.'

His eyes sparked black flame. 'I am.' Hizak folded his wings tight to his back, a statement of intent. 'I loved our dance, Marget of the Spring. I believed it had purpose. But its purpose is done. Our time has passed, just as it should. The cities are empty; you have found a better way to live.' His eyes travelled again to the desperate movements of the blinded machines. 'And their suffering will end soon enough.'

Marget's hand slipped down to take his, a gesture of comfort, and she asked of him, 'What will you do, then, Hizak of the Well?'

Hizak looked down at Marget, a faraway wistful pain crossing his face. 'Do your people not dance, Marget of the Spring?'

'They do, right enough,' she said proudly, 'but not on fire.'

'Then,' he replied, solemn and slow as the moon rising, 'I will have to teach them.'

OF ALL THINGS

LOUISE COLE

TESLA'S HANDS SHOOK as she fumbled the crystal back onto its little plinth. The old man caught her fingers, steadied her.

'Gently now,' he said.

The candlelight played around the craggy texture of the cave, glowing gold and brown on what Tesla had come to think of as its inside face. She had been scared when they first made the descent into the rock, but now she was grateful for its solid presence all around her, like an impenetrable cocoon, keeping her safe. Illusion, she knew, but a comforting one.

'How many have you done, child?' asked Marcus. He guided her to the little fire they had built in the floor.

'As many as I can remember. I don't know, I'm scared that I'm not thinking straight, that I'm losing things. Important things.' Tesla sat down on the dry earthen floor and pulled her wool chemise around her. 'I'm scared so I'm not thinking straight.'

'Of course you are scared,' said Marcus. 'Only a fool is not scared. The brave carry on, despite fear, if the job is important enough.'

Tesla nodded, and took the cup of warmed wine from Brennen with a small smile. The boy settled himself next to her.

'I want to thank you both,' Marcus said abruptly. Despite the speed of delivery, his voice cracked slightly. 'I am more grateful than you will ever know…' He winced, as if cursing his choice of words. He shook his head slightly in exasperation. 'I would not have liked to spend these final days alone.'

A small silence filled the space between them. Tesla willed herself into it, wishing she could inhabit this little sliver of eternity, never have to leave this pause, this moment between breaths.

Brennen broke it finally. 'You're welcome. But I just wanted to live. For as long as I could. To the last minute.'

Tesla looked down at the mud, packed hard into solid floor from the pressure of their feet. They were flattened too, she felt, becoming a little thinner every day, a little smaller, a little closer to being a compressed piece of nothing by the sheer weight of the end-days which had passed. How long was there? One more? Two more?

'What stories did you record?' Brennen asked.

She smiled. 'Stupid ones. My first day of school. It was the first time I had heard the tale of the word. It seemed fitting.'

He grinned. 'I remembered I had never told the story of my first love.'

Tesla spluttered into her wine. 'Your what? You're like fourteen. What great love story could you tell?'

'Oh it was a tragic tale of unrequited passion. Could rival the greats.'

Marcus smiled, and warmed his hands over the fire. 'I can think of nothing more important to lay down on the scroll of the universe than the first moment you felt love.'

Brennen nodded, sardonic quirk to his lips. 'Kind of what I thought.'

'So who was she?' Tesla tried not to sound peeved. Jealousy was ridiculous, in the circumstances, but she was jealous. She could feel its tiny pincers biting into her belly, and it rolling sinuously through her gut. Not jealous of Brennen… but of the feeling. She would have liked to know how love felt. Real love, not just for your Mum and Dad and your family, but that pulse-quickening adoration of someone new.

'Her name was Bethan and she was seven years old. She came to school every day with her fiery red hair arranged a different way — pigtails, braids, on top of her head… I don't even know what you call all the styles. Her mother must have spent hours each morning. And then one day, she came in with it loose. It just flowed there, like a visible autumn breeze or a stream of copper. And I thought I'd never seen anything so captivating in all my life.'

'A visible breeze? You thought that when you were seven?' Tesla gave up. She was irritable, and scared and jealous and angry. The feelings swept through in waves, hot and prickly becoming ice-cold and numb. She was going to die. She was right to be scared and angry and jealous, she decided. It was all so unfair.

'No,' said Brennen. 'But that's the story-telling part. It's not just… what happened. It's how you *think* about what happened.'

'But if we aren't recording truth, what's the point of this?' Tesla exclaimed, gesturing around the shining shelves of crystals. 'Why record everything into the Chandras at all, if it's not the truth about who we were? Why didn't we just lie down and die with the rest of them?'

'It is truth,' said Marcus, setting her cup of wine back on the floor. Its contents soaked into the mud like a bloody stain. 'It just isn't fact. The scientists left their data, their molecule plus molecule gives x equations. And that's great. But it isn't who we are as people. Capturing these life stories… this is our truth. This is our immortality.'

Tesla turned to the wall and ran a sharp edge of rock against her palm. It stung and then burned. She had expected a bee sting and was appalled and exhilarated to find it hurt like a knife wound, loud and vicious. She had forgotten there was so much life left in her.

'I'm sorry,' she murmured.

'S'okay,' said Brennen. 'If you can't flip out when you're going to die, when can you, I always say.' Jaunty voice, eyes liquid with fear. Being brave for her. And, just for a moment, Tesla felt a surge of something primal, an adoration and gratitude that soaked her whole being. Maybe she thought, maybe that was love. It was a nice thought.

'It seems a good time to tell the First Story,' said Marcus. 'Together. Then you can make your choices.'

Tesla's heart hiccupped in her chest. Just a tiny leap, a little thud, like the jerk of a mouse torn between running and hiding. 'Is it here? Is it now?'

The star had been growing closer to the atmosphere, sending huge waves of water over the land, and blowing gales across the dry forests. The forests in turn burned with fire that ran and skipped across the ground like sunlight at daybreak. It was a ragged, wild dance that left the land exhausted and crumpled.

Tesla had watched from the mountain before they descended into the cave. After she had left the bodies of her parents and her younger sister sleeping forever in their home, the traces of vomit from the poison carefully wiped clean, and set out with Brennen and Marcus to the Chandra cave to preserve the people's stories. She had stood on the narrow ledge for a few stolen moments and watched the world burn and drown. She could have gone with them, ended it in a few moments. But her hand wouldn't do it. Her mouth wouldn't close on the capsule.

Her story couldn't end with a vomit-stained mouth. Of all the things which should not matter, it did. If dying was all she had left, it did.

She glanced anxiously at the Chandra shelves, their facets sparkling light across the cave walls like nervous fireflies, clustering and breaking apart. She swallowed. 'Will it work?' she asked nodding toward the crystals. 'I mean, are we sure it will work?'

Marcus bit his lip before answering. She wondered if he were choosing between kindness and honesty; which was more important for the last words you ever uttered?

'I believe it will work. But I do not know.'

'Truth, not fact?' asked Brennen. He had sidled next to Tesla and viewed the crystals with wide eyes.

'Maybe. Or faith, not evidence.' Marcus took down a small crystal and turned it in his hand. Its light flickered in his eyes. 'The crystals are strange things. Did you learn in school about the signs of life?'

Tesla and Brennen nodded. 'Adaptation, reproduction, organised design… I forget the rest,' murmured Tesla.

'Response to stimuli. That's one,' said Brennen.

'Indeed,' said Marcus. 'Well I don't know if these crystals are alive. But they have an organised structure. They reproduce themselves. They drink in and conduct energy. That is how they store our words. They have adapted to their environment. But they are alive with information which is not so easily destroyed as the information in our DNA. Information stored as pure energy.' He put the Chandra back onto the shelf. 'You know they were called the librarians of creation?'

Brennen nodded. 'Because we can learn about the formation of the planet from studying the patterns in the crystals through the ages.'

Marcus smiled. 'Yes. So do I know for a fact that our stories will continue? That who we were will continue to inform the universe? No. But I believe it. And I like to think it is true.'

He took their hands. 'Come. We have just a little time to record the first and last tale of our people.'

They sat by the fire and placed the last empty Chandra on the floor between them. Marcus placed his finger on the crystal and began.

'In the beginning was the word. It enlivened the darkness and the nothing and gave the universe its name. And once it had a name, it began to know itself and to grow.'

Brennen put his finger on the crystal and repeated the words he had known since childhood. Not so very long, really. 'And as it grew, it created new words for what it was and what it would like to be. It imagined and it became.'

Tesla put her finger on the top of the crystal which glowed a soft gold. 'And parts of itself separated and found names of their own. They became plants and animals and people. They became the rocks of the mountain and the waters of the river and the shining crystals that illuminated the deep darkness at the centre of the world where no other light came. The darkness and the nothing which remained at the heart of all things and into which all things would one day return.'

Marcus glanced at the two children and nodded. They spoke the final words together. As an act of faith.

'And on that day, when the darkness rises and the nothing returns, the names will fly on crystal light into the great emptiness. And they will become once again a single word, which is the beginning and the end and the sum of all things.'

They removed their hands and the crystal glow dulled. Tesla reached for it but Marcus said: 'Leave it. It does not matter now. It will fare as well there as anywhere.' He pulled the capsules from his pocket and held them out. 'We do not have long. This will make it fast and painless.' He did not move.

Tesla raised her hand towards him but hesitated. 'I think… I think I would rather go outside. I want to see it. I want to watch.' I want to live, she meant, but she knew the words made no sense. Not now.

'As you wish.' Marcus pulled her close. 'If love means anything now, you have all of mine. Both of you.'

'I think maybe it means more now than ever,' Tesla whispered. She pulled away, turned.

'Wait.' Brennen caught her arm. 'I'll go with you.' He took her hand and held it firmly as they stepped up the narrow chiselled pathway.

The wind buffeted and punched them long before they reached the top but he didn't let go. The feeling of his fingers around hers made Tesla curiously happy.

Holding hands, they stepped out into the maelstrom and the darkness and, after a moment, the nothing swept down upon them.

****

No time. No place. No light. No thing.

And then in the darkness and the nothing there is a tremor. A tightening. An inhalation. A moment of power and intent.

And in the beginning there is a Word.

TO KILL A WOLF

STEPHEN GODDEN

'YOU'LL NOT COME WITH US, YAN?' Storac asked the man squatting beside him amongst the trees. He could hear the faint rumble of a waterfall off to their right, where the stream running through their camp poured over a cliff to the valley floor below.

Yanol's dark eyes studied the valley. He held two stones in his right hand, rotating them around each other without letting them touch. An old habit of the big barbarian; he said it helped him think. 'No, brother.' Yanol shook his shaggy head. 'Not my people down there. I'll move on.' He spoke the common tongue with a softly musical accent.

Storac nodded. 'The King's returned to his throne. We need to… to… to show…' Shame at their defeat closed up his throat; tears freed it. 'We need to show our loyalty.'

Amongst the tents and pavilions of the Kingsmen, a fire pit burned. The scent of roasting meat, hogflesh, carried to Storac's nostrils on the breeze. His stomach grumbled in reply.

'You should come with me,' Yanol said. 'My people would kill me… slowly… for fighting against my chief and failing to win.'

'We're not—' Storac cut off the words before he insulted his blood-brother. You don't call a man who clasped blood to blood with you a savage. 'It's different here, brother. They need us to return to our farms.'

Yanol snorted, tossed the two stones into the stream, and stood. He overtopped Storac by almost a head and Storac was considered tall amongst his people. Yanol glanced back at the fifty men beside their horses. Dirty, ragged, their armour mismatched and battered, but their blades clean and sharp and their horses well-fed and cared for. 'You're not farmers anymore, brother.'

'We can return to our lands, our families, our people.' Storac took a deep breath. 'We have to show loyalty or the King'll harry our lands to extinction.'

'Land is land, people are people, and the two don't marry. One just lives upon the other for a while.'

'That's not our way.'

'I know.' Yanol stretched. 'I'll come back this way some day and see how you are getting on.' He smiled. 'You have daughters?'

'Two of them, be eight and nine by now, pretty as buttons.'

'I'll see you in ten summers then.' Yanol grinned with strong white teeth.

'I'd gut you like a fish.' Storac tried to grin in return, but failed.

'Might be worth it.' Yanol clapped a huge hand on Storac's shoulder. 'Glad I didn't kill you, brother.'

Storac sighed. 'I had ten men with me. You were half dead out there in the wasteland. Frozen and bleeding. You couldn't have killed a bedraggled rat.'

'Aye. So you keep saying.' Yanol turned to Moran, Storac's cousin, holding the reins of two horses in one meaty fist. 'Look after him, keep him out of fights with the Kingsmen; they'll be itching to prove their worth against Storac the Wolf.'

'I'll do that, Yan,' Moran said. 'Where'll you go?'

'Across the mountains. See what's on the other side.'

'They say there's a dragon up there.'

Yanol touched the longsword strapped to his back. 'Best it stays out of my way then.'

****

Down on the valley floor, amongst the Kingsmen waiting to receive the rebels, Belazrin the sorcerer whispered to his elemental allies in a language filled with the crackle of flames. His mind itched with the power needed to keep them small, hidden, without form, while they struggled to escape, to flare, to ride the air towards the ragged group of rebel cavalry trotting out of the forest.

'Wait,' Belazrin whispered. 'Wait. Let them draw in. Let them become fodder.' No other in this camp could understand what he said; few could even recognise it as language.

To Kill A Wolf

In the tongue of flame, his allies hissed their compliance to his power. The pressure eased on Belazrin's mind and he breathed out a sigh. So hard to control such powerful elementals. Strong amongst their kind, but then Belazrin was strong amongst his.

Twenty of the King's soldiers wandered about the camp, keeping up appearances, to lull the rebels into the trap. They thought to kill the Wolf and his pack. Belazrin resisted the urge to giggle.

To kill a wolf, one must first bait the trap and the bait rarely survives the encounter.

'Wait.'

'What was that, wizard?' Vron Halstead slapped his gauntlets against his thigh.

'I do not speak to you,' Belazrin snapped. Wizard indeed. The fool thought all magic alike. Belazrin was no wise man snuffling about with scrolls and runes. He tapped into the source of all magic, the elements themselves. Fire, air, water, earth, but it was fire he loved, fire warmed his cold soul and comprehended his rages.

Vron Halstead shivered, then hid his unease with hatred. 'Look at them. Dirty, stinking, traitorous scum, riding tall in the saddle like they're nobles about the hunt.'

'Calm yourself,' Belazrin said, his voice soft as a wind chime. He heard the call returned from his other allies above the valley. The elementals of the air wished only to strike. 'They must not see your hate.'

'Their wives and daughters will feel my hate deep within them,' Vron Halstead said. 'Deep within them,' he repeated softly.

Belazrin could smell the man's lust upon the breeze. Vron Halstead had raped his way through the war, so the King found it politic to have him killed. Brutalising women of noble birth, albeit supporters of the rebels, mandated recourse from a royal court regaining its power. Not all of Vron Halstead's victims died and their vengeance required answer.

Storac the Wolf lifted one hand and his men spread out across the valley floor, almost as if they were about to start another of those wild charges for which they were justly feared.

Vron Halstead grunted his displeasure and said, 'That big ox of a barbarian isn't with them.'

'No matter. The Galae know only battle. He would have gone on his way. No war here left to fight.'

The fire elementals rustled flame-tinged words of impatience and spite.

'Wait,' Belazrin said in the tongue of flame. 'A little longer. The gifts are almost here.'

'That's a demonic tongue.' Vron Halstead shivered again and twisted his fingers around his thumb in a warding gesture.

That would not save him.

As before, Vron Halstead returned to vicious wishful thinking when faced with the sounds of Belazrin speaking to things he could neither see nor hear. 'Would have liked to have sunk my blade into his guts. Deep within.' He shook himself alert. 'He killed too many of the nobility to be left alive. We'll have to hunt him now.'

'You'll not be able to track a Galae. Not in the wild lands. The King will send assassins against him. Not soldiers.'

The rebels halted their horses twenty paces from the camp. Storac the Wolf dismounted, tossed his reins to one of his men and advanced on foot towards Vron Halstead and Belazrin.

The scars on the rebel's face, on his arms, told of his long struggle against his rightful King. His left hand rested on the ruby hilt of his sword to keep the long blade at his waist from tangling with his legs. His helm rested in the crook of his right arm and his long copper-blond hair, bound into a tight knot at the base of his skull, where it would lay under the mail coif and cushion blows to the back of his neck, shone in the sunlight.

'I'm Storac,' he called, his voice strong despite the humiliation. 'I've come to pledge allegiance to the throne.'

Belazrin waited until all the rebels had dismounted. Then he released the firedance.

****

Yanol rasped the whetstone along the blade of his double-edge long-sword and kept his gaze on the valley below. He should go, the sun was already low in the sky, but he waited to see his blood-brother safely received back into the slave life these people called civilisation.

He sniffed the air. A tainted scent swirled upon the breeze and raised the hairs on the back of his neck. He touched the vambrace on his left arm where the armour covered the bracelet.

That taint, like fire upon the grassland, like the heat of a forge shimmering the air, like the hissing stench of fire-rocks dropping into the sea. Magic afoot here, not the magic of a shaman to bind the oath Storac was about to give — this tasted of flame. Yanol sheathed the longsword and picked up the saddle beside his horse. A good horse, Bregas, a black coat, with three white socks, strong-bodied, short-legged, built for the mountains.

As he pulled tight the twin cinch-straps around Bregas's belly, Yanol looked down into the valley.

The rebels dismounted. Storac walked forward. The leader of the Kingsmen lifted his arm. Who was that beside him? That was no shaman.

That smell, almost unknown in the lands of Yanol's birth. Sorcerers who meddled with the elements did not live long amongst the Galae. Too dangerous, the elementals wild, without morality or compassion, unadulterated creatures of chaotic nature, who sought only to be unleashed upon this world.

Yanol swung onto the back of Bregas, kicked the horse into motion, and charged down the slope towards the abomination of elemental sorcery.

The trees obscured the valley floor for long moments. Bregas clattered down the treacherous path.

Too late.

Flames exploded into the air above the trees.

The crackling song of fire roared through his ears, but Yanol kicked at Bregas's sides. The horse tried to fight his urging, but Yanol forced him onwards, downwards, towards his blood-brother's need.

****

Belazrin laughed for the joy of it all.

Fire danced amongst the rebels. The elementals spinning like tops between the screaming men. Skipping from fire pit, to human, to horse. Flames flared where they touched. Hair caught alight in an instant, men screamed. Horses bolted, their manes, their tails afire, liquid flame dripping upon the grass.

And still the fire danced.

And sang.

In roaring tongues of flame.

The music crackled, popped, caught updrafts and curled along the melody. It shimmered, it simmered, it cooked all scent from the air. Nothing left but the heat, the crisping of nostril hairs, the blazing agony digging into the flesh of men.

However, Storac did not stop moving, did not start screaming, did not die.

Despite the song of the flames, the dance of the fire, the magnitude of the heat, he staggered towards Belazrin with his skin on fire. The stench of roasting flesh burst through the pure smell of the flames — such a human smell to corrupt such purity, thought Belazrin. Storac's heated armour blistered his skin and still he lurched forward. The skin around his knuckles blackened, flaking away where it clutched the hilt of his upraised sword. His mouth closed. Not breathing, for to inhale would be to fill his lungs with flame. Squinting through eyelids scorched clean of lashes, trying to preserve his sight for long enough. Knowing he was already dead, but stumbling towards the sorcerer anyway.

Belazrin watched the approach of the burning man with interest. How did he keep moving? His sinews must be starting to shrink in the intense heat.

Vron Halstead drew his sword, laughed, and said, 'So the honour falls to me, Wolf.'

Storac stumbled to one knee and could not rise again. His mouth opened for the last time, his last breath. 'I curse you.' The fire poured down his throat along with his breath and he crumpled to the ground.

'A pity,' Vron Halstead said.

'Yes.' Belazrin brought his hands together and cried out in a voice like wind chimes. 'Unleash yourselves.' The clap of his hands echoed along the valley. Thrice more he clapped.

The wind elementals roared down from the mountaintops where they had been gathering density from the coldness. Falling faster, faster, towards the flames of their fire-kin.

'What, they're all dead,' Vron Halstead cried out. 'All dead!'

'Not all, my dear rapist lord,' Belazrin said.

'I'm a captain for my King.'

'You raped women related to the royal family.'

'They were traitors.'

'They were noble. You should have stuck to farm girls.'

'But I could be useful…!' Vron Halstead shrieked, but the wind hit anyway, lifting him, throwing him into the fire, flushing the flames with oxygen, flash-burning his body, the bodies of his men, their horses, their tents. In the middle of the conflagration, Belazrin stood, untouched, laughing.

****

The trees saved Yanol's life.

And Bregas.

The horse flattened his ears, reared, plunged, jumped four-legged into the air, when the supercooled air whistled through the trees. Yanol kept his seat, grabbed handfuls of reins, shortened his grip, tried to pull the horse's head around. Bregas, with foam-flecked lips, terror in his rolling eyes, tried to slam the maniac on his back against a tree.

Yanol swung his left leg out of the stirrup and over the back of the horse, just in time to avoid it being crushed between horseflesh and tree bark, but now he was off balance, clinging to the saddle-horn. Bregas rolled towards him, dropping, intending to squash Yanol beneath his body. Yanol had no choice; he leapt clear of the horse, hit the ground, tumbled away.

Bregas, his tail high, bolted back up the slope.

The wave of heat and flame lashed upwards from the valley floor. Yanol covered his eyes with his left arm. The tops of the trees caught aflame, but the trunks, so closely packed together, shielded Yanol from the intensity of the heat.

His comrades were dead, his blood-brother Storac was dead, none could survive such an inferno. The charmed bracelet protected Yanol from direct attacks of magic, but this heat was mundane, physical not spiritual. He lunged onto his feet and sprinted up the slope.

Pushing hard, arms pumping, legs thrusting against the soft ground, Yanol charged up the hill. His thigh muscles bunched and released, breath gasped into his throat, the sword on his back bounced around, its hilt striking the side of his head, but he could not spare the hand to hold it steady. He needed both his arms pumping, helping his feet to move faster over the ground, to climb the slope, to get to the water before the fire came for him.

Flames licked along the trunks of the trees, blazing branches fell all about him, but he did not stop, did not look up. He hurdled fires started in his path by embers dripping from the trees above. He twisted past branches burning on the ground where they fell. He closed his throat against the thick, black, glutinous smoke.

And raced up the slope, towards the stream, towards the waterfall.

Skipping across the tops of the trees, fire elementals chased him for no more reason than that they could.

****

Belazrin sighed a deep happy sigh. Lassitude flowed through his veins. Exhaustion threatened, but he had one task left to do.

He surveyed the scorched earth around him. Nothing left of the camp, the humans, or their beasts except melted lumps of metal. Air and fire made for such a strong heat. The forest burned around the slopes of the valley. A fire he would have to quench before it raged out of control beyond the valley walls.

The fire elementals had left his side, but the air elementals swirled around him still. All was good, all was under his control. He called forth the elementals of water with liquid tones, subtle melodies. They spun out of the river, where the path to their world lay, and allowed the winds to lift them, high, high above the blazing forest. Sucking in moisture as they rose.

Roiling clouds above the flames.

****

Yanol threw himself through the curtain of the waterfall with the heat of the fire elementals on his neck. They hissed as the water behind him turned to steam.

Flickering tongues of flame darted between the elementals as they laid their plans. Yanol stood with his back flat against the rock of the falls, the water cascading past his face. He could not drive them back to where they belonged; he had little skill with magic. His was the way of sword and bow. The bracelet would not help him against these creatures.

He filled his lungs with moist air and prepared to sing his death chant. He drew his sword and prepared to die in battle. He did not bother to call upon his gods, because they had never helped him in the past.

Rain lashed down beyond the curtain of the waterfall. The fire-elementals screeched; a sound like hot metal quenched in blood.

The flash of flame blazed white heat into this world. Yanol turned his face away from the glare of the curtain ripping between the world of the elementals and the world of man. The fire elementals fled, but the elemental rain continued to quench the fire their brethren had started.

****

Belazrin cast the final spell, sending the water elementals home, and slumped to the ground exhausted. The exhilaration of his spell-casting faded away and he could not speak, could not move. Lethargy weighted down his arms, his legs. His powers depleted, he sprawled upon the ash-covered ground.

A wagon trundled into the valley in a jingle of horse brasses. Belazrin lay, unable to speak, waiting for his servant to approach.

'Such mighty power, master,' Volk the servant said. 'The flames rose like curtains against the sky.' Squat Volk lifted Belazrin in mighty arms and placed him upon the mattress in the bed of the wagon. 'Sleep now, master, I'll see us home safe.'

He turned the wagon and soon all lay silent again upon the ash-strewn scene.

****

The valley stank of fire, of charred wood and roasted earth. Evening twilight cast long shadows over the devastated landscape. The ash of trees, soaked by the rain, clung to Yanol's boots. He stamped to clear the caustic substance from the leather and then strode out across the ash of grass, of earth, of humans. An ash that burned the mind, not the flesh.

He walked amongst the dead, barely even bones left and those crumbling to the touch. Melted iron all that remained of swords and armour. Yanol scanned the ground as he strode, looking for the one thing that might identify the place where his blood-brother fell.

Storac's dragon-steel sword lay upon the ground. Bent by the heat, ruined by it, but still recognisably a sword. Dragon-steel did not melt like other metals did, but not even that wondrous metal could stand the focused heat of fire and air elementals in concert. No material can remain untouched when that which made it seeks to destroy it.

Yanol already wore a dragon-steel blade upon his back and had no need for another. So, when he killed the noble who carried that sword into battle, he'd gifted the blade to his brother. The solid ruby in the pommel of the naked hilt the final confirmation of who lay here.

He lifted the ruined blade from the ash.

Avenge me.

Scalded by the voice, he dropped the blade.

Avenge me, brother.

'Do not ask this, Storac!' Yanol cried. 'He is a sorcerer, a man of magic, with elementals at his beck and call. I will see your family to safety. I will see your people to another land. But do not ask this of me.'

Avenge me.

Yanol's shoulders slumped. He nodded his head. 'For all that we were, I will do this, brother, but you do not know what you ask.' He took a breath. 'Eternity is a long time, Storac.'

Avenge me.

'I will.' Yanol unclenched his fists and, kneeling, ran the edge of his dagger across the palms of his hands. He lifted the crumbling bone that had once been Storac's skull. He crushed it to dust with his bare hands. His blood and sweat mingled with the dust, the grey, gritty dust that had once been his blood-brother. He packed the dust into a leather sack, scouring the ground, retrieving all the bones and adding them to the grey, sticky mess within the sack. Finally, he prised the heat-dulled ruby from its mount upon the hilt and dropped it into the sack along with the bone-ash of Storac.

'This may take some time, brother.'

Avenge me.

****

Anna, Storac's grieving wife, saw the world through the red lace of a widow. Her children skipped around the wagon she guided along the path Yanol marked with short stakes.

Yanol had arrived in the night with word of her husband's death. He brought together all the peoples of the outlying farms.

And gave them gold. 'I met a tax-collector on the road,' was all he would say on the matter.

That very night, in wagons piled high with all their worldly possessions, the families of Storac's Wolves fled from their land.

Across the rolling plains, heading south east, days, weeks, months passed. Yanol scouted ahead on his black horse with three white socks. Sometimes, Yanol returned with injuries, wounds, but no attacker ever bothered the wagon train of fifty families travelling across the plains. Eldest sons grew into men on that journey, learned their ways from Yanol and the old grey-heads who remembered what it used to be like.

Until, finally, this sun-kissed day, Yanol led them to this valley.

'The people of these hills are hospitable, friendly; they will welcome you here amongst them. This valley has good soil, good drainage, you can grow crops here.'

'Won't they mind that we take their land?' Anna asked.

'They do not consider this land to be theirs and you should not name it yours either. This is just land, Anna, it belongs to no-one. Tend it, plant your crops, raise your families, but do not call this land yours for you do not own it. Call it your home instead.' Yanol swung himself up onto the back of Bregas. 'The people of these hills call themselves Eloni; their women will come to your camp tonight. Welcome them. Feed them. And their men will come tomorrow.'

'Where do you go, Yanol?' Anna cried out, tearing the widow's lace from her head.

Bregas stamped the ground, turning in a tight circle, eager to run. Yanol sat in the saddle with native grace. 'I go to keep a promise to the spirit of your husband.'

'Will you pass this way again?' Anna asked.

'You'll see me again, one day, if I survive and you survive, Anna wife of Storac — brother of my blood. If you have need of me, tell the Eloni. They have magic that can call across a thousand leagues.' Yanol gave Bregas his head and galloped away.

****

Yanol tossed the bundle onto the cave floor, 'Come out, Flasak, I have trade for you.'

A light flared in the dark of the cave and the necromancer Flasak stepped out of the shadows. 'Ho, Yanol Stormrider, son of Canan, son of Melana, wanderer, warrior, grey-cloaked killer of serpents.'

'Ho, Flasak Shadowmancer, born to a race now extinguished and last of your kin, death seducer, loremaster of the old ways, brother to none, friend to the dead.' Yanol bowed his head ever so slightly, but did not take his gaze from the creature revealed.

Flasak had once been human, but now he lived in shadow and darkness, his skin bleached pale for the lack of sunlight upon it, sagging from his skeletal frame in folds of opalescent flesh. Colours shimmered as he moved. A band of god-iron welded across his eyes, Flasak could not see as mortals see, but he could see through the shroud of death to that which lay beyond.

'You carry a spirit with you, Yanol,' Flasak said.

'I do. A man betrayed and burned to ash in the flame of an elemental fire.'

'A sorcerer's treachery knows no boundaries for they are less than human, living always with the scheming of their elemental familiars in their minds.'

Yanol laughed. 'Such as you talks of humanity?'

'I live amongst death, blade-sworn Yanol of the Galae. That makes me more human than most. What lies in yonder bundle?'

'The heart, brain, and spinal chord of a werebeast I met upon the road.' Yanol rubbed at the scar upon his face, a scar caked with the remnants of the wood ash used to burn out the poison of the curse before it passed to Yanol.

'A rare gift.'

'A trade.' Yanol's jaw tightened.

'What do you wish?'

'To kill a sorcerer.'

Flasak studied Yanol's face for a moment, then nodded sadly. 'Vengeance has a cost; will your spirit-friend pay the price?'

Yes, whispered Storac's soul.

****

Volk, servant to the sorcerer Belazrin, enjoyed his time off amongst the whores and braggarts of the dockyards. His knuckles blooded, his lusts satisfied, he hitched up his breeches and went looking for a drink.

'Volk,' the voice hissed out of an alley.

He turned, his fists raised in front of his face, his eyes squinting into the shadows. He spat upon the earth and snarled, 'Who's there?'

His last words.

****

Belazrin woke in his rooms in the palace. He sniffed the air. That smell? It excited him. He opened his eyes. Darkness surrounded him. What had awoken him? A dream? Was he dreaming still?

He reached out a hand, intending to light the candle beside his bed with a little touch of elemental flame. Pain gripped his arm, a spasm of agony, running from his pointed finger to the point of his shoulder.

That smell.

The pain faded and his arm dropped upon the blankets. Something sticky, cold, smelling of death, coated his arm.

'The ash of a firestorm, left behind by a dance let loose upon this world,' a voice said in the darkness. 'That is what sorcerers call a group of fire elementals, is it not? A dance? That firestorm blasted with the air of a choir of air elementals, such heat when such creatures dance together; that firestorm extinguished by a babble of water elementals. Powerful magic.'

'Who is there?'

'The ash of a man burned by fire and air, drenched by water, mixed with earth. The ash of a man who died cursing you with his last breath.'

'Storac.'

'No fire will come to you here. No water. No air. No earth. Your powers fail you, sorcerer.'

'How?'

'Blood, Belazrin. Lots and lots of blood. My people know how to deal with sorcerers. You made it easier for me with your extravagance. Three of the four elementals mixed into the ash. I only had to have earth added to the mix. Then I just had to find the blood of somebody you cared about to bind it all.'

'Volk.'

'Your servant. I bled him like a pig.'

'You're a savage.'

'So they say.'

'You're that barbarian Yanol.'

'Yes.' Yanol flung the shutters back from the window. Moonlight flooded the room.

'You have some spell left? Something to kill me with? Some spell of moonlight?' Belazrin could see the huge form of the barbarian outlined against the window.

'No. I just needed the light so you could see. Catch.'

An object flew towards Belazrin's face. He caught it without thinking and looked at it, some sort of jewel. 'What is this?'

I curse you.

The heat flared from the ruby, the room flooded with light, Belazrin screamed. The fire danced across the blood-mixed ash strewn across his bed, his room, his skin.

****

Yanol jogged away from the palace as the flames lit up the night sky behind him. The fire elementals would dance until dawn, the air elementals would sing their song into the heat, and then at dawn water and earth would put out the flames. A magic more powerful than sorcery guided their actions.

The King would die here with all his entourage; vengeance for a dead rebel would plunge the land into civil war again.

'You will be trapped here now, my brother.' Yanol said. 'This is old magic, built upon the soul, upon death. There is nothing I can do to release your soul.'

I am content.

'Goodbye, Storac the Wolf, brother of blood. I'll not pass this way again.'

Fire Starter

Jae Erwin

MAYBE THIS WILL MAKE THE NEWS.

The fizz of excitement ran up Caleb's arms and down into his chest. His heart thumped hard against his rib cage. He liked the way his fast breath made him feel more alive.

A sulphur tang of struck matches stung Caleb's nose as he poked another through the small triangle between twigs, into the ball of paint-soaked rags at the centre. He'd stolen them from outside a builder's hut. Pushing up through his arms, off his belly, to his feet, Caleb pulled his sweat-damp t-shirt from his shoulders and stepped back. He took care not to stumble over the hummocked brown moorland grass, the strands so dry they fractured as his trainers met them.

Flames leapt from rags to wood to grass with a satisfying crackle. The fourth fire in a short line across the hillside above the old mill lodge. Fire-starting was something of a talent, perhaps his only one. Caleb knew where to place starting materials and how to make best use of a breeze without losing his eyebrows and fringe.

His mum didn't even notice that first time, stupid bitch; too spaced out on pills to see the frazzled, crunchy hair-ends turned ginger. She'd have seen it if she'd needed him to cadge something off the neighbours: milk, bread, margarine.

Caleb's stomach clenched as hard as his fists, remembering the pity, or being-taken-for-a-ride suspicion in their eyes. And that dirty git at number seven who'd wanted payback for the freebies when he was younger. So he made sure they didn't run out of things anymore.

Ha, he was wrong; fire-starting wasn't his only talent. A surprise burst of humour extinguished the burn of poverty-shame. Shoplifting's another skill. Always buy something small when nicking; smile politely, play nice.

He kept a slush fund of a quid, a tactical reserve for his forays, well away from his mother's thieving hands.

He should audition for 'Britain's Got Talent'.

He smirked as he hitched his trackies over his hip bones, rolled twice at the top to stop them falling down. The bag of jumble his mother pinched from the church porch came up trumps last time. The pants almost fit him. Better than the usual contents — cast-off baby clothes and old lamp shades. Caleb pushed away the corrosive bitterness of a life of hand-me-downs, unemployment and living with his mother, using the bravado of living on the edge.

Flames ran ahead of the wind, a wriggling line of orange outraced by blue smoke, and left a growing patch of black desolation behind.

Time to leave; before a dog walker turns up and dobs him in.

Caleb picked up his Dad's old fishing rod, his excuse for being up there if anyone asked, and headed towards the tight stand of trees to watch. The danger of being caught rippled along his nerves, chased by the thrill of the chance to watch the fire brigade battle his handiwork, maybe even help them.

****

Stripped down to fireproof pants and t-shirts, just the way she liked them — well, almost. Lilith leaned back against the wind-blasted trunk of a hawthorn tree, eyeing up the sooty figures beating out the flames.

Once upon a time they'd have been naked to the waist, not now; health and safety had a lot to answer for. Her bottom lip stuck out.

She flicked her gaze to the side, chewed her lip, fondly remembering earlier times, and caught a fragment of movement in the trees. Lilith rolled her body away from the trunk in an undulating S-curve, sauntered past a firefighter and trailed a finger along exposed skin where t-shirt had broken free of pants. The firewoman jerked up and whipped her head around, her sweaty fringe curled against her forehead.

Can't see what's right behind you? Stupid human. Lilith edged around the fire.

There, who's that watching? Skinny... but quite pretty if you like blue eyes with dark hair. Male.

Lilith weaved towards the hawthorn and hazel thicket.

Let's see what he's up to. Ah! Firestarter. Killing the grass and all the little creatures? What fun could she have with — she froze as his thin face turned towards her.

Oooo, a sensitive. He knew she was there — even better. She could play with this one.

****

Caleb allowed the toes of his trainers to scrape along the spongy tarmac with each return sweep of the swing.

What did he see up on the moors yesterday? Not a heat shimmer from the flames; it was in the wrong place for that.

A ghost? Don't they have to be in buildings?

What about an alien?

His breathing rate spiked and he launched himself off the swing and across the playground, trying to mask his fear with action. He'd read an old copy of Communion that he'd found in a jumble bag a couple of months back, and scared the shit out of himself. The front cover on its own was enough: an elongated alien face with coal-black eyes.

'Hello, Caleb.'

'Aagh.' His shout rang one note short of a girly scream but he was too scared to care. He jumped round in a circle. 'Who are you…? Where are you, for fuck's sake?'

'Right here.' The voice oozed like melted chocolate.

He leapt again as a puff of air blew in his ear. 'Stop it. Leave me alone.'

'Can't do that Caleb. You've been a naughty boy.'

Caleb's breathing hit sprint levels and he rocketed over the tarmac and onto the grass, heading toward the backs of the council houses. He pumped his arms and legs, the muscles burning, and tried to breathe around the stitch in his side.

'Oh no you don't.'

Caleb bounced off nothing and landed on his back on the hard-baked lawn with a thump that knocked all the air out of his lungs. Gulping in air, he fought like a feral cat to get up but only his head and neck moved. Everything else weighted to the ground by… nothing.

'Lie still!'

'Get off me!' Caleb screamed and the sounds smacked him back in the face as if he'd yelled into a bucket.

'No-one can hear you. Now calm down. I want to talk to you. Nothing more.'

'Fuck, fuck, fuck,' Caleb panted, his ribcage punching down into his belly and sweat rolling down his face like tears.

The shape of a woman formed in front of him. Even in his panic his stomach melted into hot liquid and plummeted to his balls as his whole system registered her curves. He groaned and let his head fall back.

'If I ease off on the body control will you walk with me? To somewhere I don't have to keep up this screen?'

Caleb nodded. His hormones got the better of his brain.

'I'm Lilith.' She held out her hand.

He snatched his hand to his side, fist clenched. 'Are you an alien?'

'No, but I'm about to change your sorry little life.'

He glanced down at his second-hand clothes. This time he took her offered hand.

****

Caleb paced to and from the window in his bedroom, floorboards creaking with every other step.

She seemed real enough: red hair to her waist and legs to die for, but how did he know she wasn't a delusion? That's what the doctors said about his Dad. He really believed what he saw and heard: before he killed himself.

Caleb reached his bed again and launched himself onto it. He squirmed one way then another.

He refused to think about his Dad, flung himself onto his side and turned his back to the room.

Imagine having super-powers though. Lilith said he could stick with fire as the main channel, since that's what he was good at. She's fuckin' hot too. He wondered would she…

'Hello again, Caleb.'

His body jerked in a single massive twitch. 'Shit. Will you stop doing that?'

'What?'

'Sneaking up on me. How long have you been here?' His feet rumpled the quilt as he scrambled up to sitting. The tops of Lilith's breasts, peeping out of her body-hugging top, sat like rounded cup-cakes straight out of the oven, soft and golden. Directly in his line of sight.

'Not long, why? You got something to hide?' The mattress dipped as she sat and eased closer to him.

'No!' Heat flashed to his face as he shuffled further along the bed from her. Shit, he hadn't blushed in years.

'Have you decided?' She slid a little closer and Caleb itched to move again. 'Do you want to learn how to use the life force that's all around you?'

Caleb rubbed at the bead of sweat trickling in the small of his back. 'What if I'm a raving lunatic? How do I know you're not in my head?'

'You're not and I'm not.' Lilith put a slim finger to her lips and tapped; Caleb tried not to stare and swallowed hard. 'What if I gave you a demonstration? Something to prove I'm real.'

Caleb took a deep breath. No, she can't mean…

'You like fire. Shall I set something alight for you?'

She didn't mean sex; Caleb squashed his disappointment. 'Would it be on the telly?' Then his survival instinct forced its way past the tumble of images of fame and the hormonal brain fog. 'What's in it for you?'

'Friendship; I get lonely sometimes.'

Well, he knew that one.

****

Lilith eased her behind into a rounded dip in the trunk of a fallen tree. She loved the female form. 'We'll start your training here.' The soft moss held her curves.

'What kind of training?' Caleb dragged his eyes up to her face. He had plonked himself down in the grass shining green in the tiny glade. The sunlight shimmied past the horizontal layers of beech and hornbeam leaves.

'Training to tap into the life force.' Lilith breathed in the warm air full of dancing insects and the scents of woodland. In that moment she connected consciously with the patterns, aware of the physical edges of herself, every microscopic indentation between cells, molecules, atoms, energies. 'Everything is made up of a vortex — do you know what a vortex is?'

Caleb rolled his eyes at her. 'Yeah, d'uh — I have seen Youtube you know. Things like tornados and water spouts — they both create a vortex.'

'Right. Well, everything, absolutely everything, is a unique blend of information, energy and matter.' Lilith closed her eyes. 'And the universal, fundamental form around which this organises is the spiral, the vortex.'

She could hear Caleb fidgeting. 'Sit in a position that is comfortable for you. One you can stay in for a while.' The swish of grass being swept aside by his feet and the minute shifting of the tree trunk told her Caleb had moved to lean against it beside her.

She extended her energies and opened to receive. Caleb's field pushed into hers like a hand pressed into dough; his cross-legged shape, back against the trunk, close to her calves.

'Close your eyes… Take your attention to your heart…' Lilith directed her own energy to enfold his. At first, she synchronised to his chaotic frequencies, then she slowly manipulated the wavelengths… to those that connected to the rhythms of this universe… and he followed.

Breathe into that space…

Between the waves of energy and matter…

Follow your breath in and breath out…'

Lilith sensed all the layers in him joining the pulse of her energies.

He's ready to start.

****

Caleb stared into space, across the kitchen table from his mother in her grimy, bobbled dressing gown. He crunched on his toast.

She watched him over the top of her coffee mug. 'What are you doing today?'

Her gravelly voice with a hint of whine cut through him; her anxiety tablets hadn't kicked in yet.

Should he tell her the truth?

He spent at least two hours a day now, more if he could wangle it, up in the woods and the fields practising, since Lilith had done her stuff. One touch of her finger to his forehead had cold-burned deep into his brain.

'That's your pineal gland,' Lilith had told him. 'Focus your senses between your eyes and into the centre of your brain… there, that's it, like a tiny pine cone.'

Caleb experienced himself as a plughole spiral within a hurricane, coupled together so that he'd had no choice but to rotate in synchrony; lost in a repeating weave of energy.

He'd come back to himself in the glade. The sunshine had moved on and goose pimples drew the hairs on his arms to attention.

'That's your first lesson.' Lilith had knelt so close he could smell her; wild garlic, wet wood and a note below the surface that made his pores open to take in more. 'I want you to practise the meditation each day. Open to whatever is there — exactly as it is. We'll have another lesson tomorrow.'

Caleb had struggled to withdraw his heightened senses. 'What about fire? I thought you said I'd be learning about fire.'

'Fire is simply one form. I teach you the basics of life energy first and with that you can manipulate many forms.' Lilith had been adamant.

Caleb brought his thoughts back to his mother. No, she wouldn't believe him, she'd call the doctors. 'I'm going round to Shaun's.' She wouldn't question him spending hours playing on Shaun's Xbox, but she'd be suspicious of him walking the hills and woodland.

She measured him with her pale blue eyes. 'Something's different… Did you get laid?'

'Mum!' The chair legs screeched across the lino, protesting on his behalf, as he shoved his chair back.

'Just asking. It's what mums are supposed to do, in't it?'

No it fucking isn't, Caleb wanted to scream in her face. Instead he crossed the room in two strides and catching the door in his hand slammed it into the frame after himself. The crash didn't quite cover his mother's laughter. Toast stuck in a lump at the base of his throat as he left home.

He ran up the hill and into the woods hoping it would burn off his anger. Lilith had told him strong emotions would throw up a barrier to his practice and he wanted to be calm before she got there for his lesson. He entered their glade and flung himself to the ground beside the fallen tree trunk.

Slow your breathing.

Focus on one point — inside of nostrils.

Breathe in.

Breathe out.

Anger.

Breathe in.

Breathe out.

Anger.

Breathe in.

Breathe out.

He slipped through the interface between energy and matter.

Crackle.

Caleb opened his eyes. A small yellow fire danced by his toes. 'Whoa.' He leapt to his feet and stamped on it.

'Oi! What you doing?' A bloke the size of a tractor strode up, so close to him that Caleb took a step back and tilted his head up to meet the fierce gaze blazing from under the dirty flat cap.

'Nothing. I'm… bird watching.'

'You better not be lighting fires.' The man looked down at the ground trying to see where the flames had been. Caleb had his foot on the sooty black mark.

'I'm not. That'd be mad when everything's this dry.'

The man leant forward, his squinting glance darting between Caleb's eyes. 'Don't be cocky with me, son, I can smell the smoke.'

'Is there a problem?' Lilith's hips rolled from side to side as she strolled towards them. The man's jaw dropped and he sent a wave of grasping heat sweeping towards her; Caleb staggered. On the outside looking in, he could see the play of energies, the currents, the eddies. The man's lust hit a solid wall of rejection.

'Er… er… I thought I saw flames…'

'I'm sure my friend here wouldn't do something so irresponsible. He's a nature-lover…' Lilith rolled her upper body in a whisper of a figure of eight.

'I… I… I must have made a mistake. Maybe it was the sun glinting off something. Right, well, I'll go then.' The man hunched his shoulders and tramped off into the trees, the current of lust trailing behind him.

'Where did the flames come from?' Fear and excitement trembled side by side in Caleb's gut. Did he do that?

'It seems you've skipped ahead of today's lesson all by yourself.'

Lilith's dark eyes fixed on him. 'Tell me what happened.'

There was no arguing with the command in her voice; he described how his anger-powered breath pierced the minute spaces and channelled the flames.

'You're ready to begin focusing then. To have a goal in mind.'

Fear swelled, squeezing his throat. 'What goal?'

'Destruction — of your enemies.'

****

Lilith watched as Caleb disappeared past the dark sweeping skirts of a clump of hawthorn allowed to grow without the slashing of farmers and council workers.

He had the power, maybe even more than she thought.

She twirled her finger gently against a stem of grass so that it entwined and stroked her. She returned the caress with soft brushes of dancing molecules and love.

'Don't worry little one, I'll return the pain he inflicted on your brethren up on the moors.'

The stem uncoiled in a whiplash.

****

Shifting between the spaces, spiralling through the molecules, Caleb came to the place of greatest potential for his purpose — the colours, shapes and movement which screamed *flammable*. In the world he used to call real, he crouched in the shadows of the bins of number seven. The only thing visible from beneath his hoodie, dark grey with no distinguishing logos, was the tip of his nose.

He breathed slow and steady as his mind-soul set each entangled particle to spinning faster. The excitation grew and within seconds the bottle of whiskey on the floor, near the armchair in number seven, burst into flames, sending burning glass fragments to settle on carpets, cushions and curtains. Once Caleb saw the little fires take hold and spread, he shifted the boundaries that he called self, enfolding and retreating into the envelope of flesh huddled in the dark.

'Nice work.'

For once, he didn't jump. He'd been aware of Lilith's presence from the moment she joined him. 'The slimy bastard deserves it: kiddy fiddler!'

She ignored his righteousness. 'With more practice you'll be able to do this from a distance, increase your range, but it's a good start.'

****

Third fire: Police hunt arsonist.

The newspaper billboards screamed at him from outside every corner shop. Each time, Caleb darted glances at the people around; girls in flip-flops, shorts and vest t-shirts, work men with lobster pink shoulders, camouflage cut-offs and builder's boots, and little old ladies in woolly coats despite the heat.

Can they tell it's me?

He turned the corner onto his street and almost bumped into the sicko from number seven. The creep swung a bin bag in danger of tearing into the boot of a taxi. It joined a battered suitcase and half a dozen Asda bags. He turned to Caleb. 'Going to stay at me sister's for a bit. Until t'council sorts this bloody mess out.' David — that was the dirty bastard's name — flicked his head towards the cream-fronted semi with billows of soot smudged above the two windows.

Awareness that *someone* had tried to kill him flickered in the man's eyes, but no suspicion of who; the certain knowledge of why hovered between them. David dropped his eyes first and turned back down the short path. He wasn't old and creepy like they're supposed to be, paedophiles. He was probably only ten years older than Caleb.

Caleb felt sick. He stepped into the road and round the taxi. He thought it'd feel good, getting his own back; same as burning the English block at school. All they ever did there was tell him how useless he was. And the bakery where they laughed at him when he asked if they'd any jobs. Bastards. The news said they'd be closed for a month. But this…

'That copper said there are similarities between the fires…' A group of neighbours congregated outside his house swapping snippets. 'He told me they'll be putting out a picture of someone soon…' Two of the women were still in their dressing gowns — had probably taken their kids to school in them.

Same as his mum. She'd still be in hers, too.

Caleb pushed his key into the lock — sticking as usual — and misjudged the force required to open the door, slamming it back against the wall, making the dint in the plaster a little bit bigger.

'Stop banging that bloody door will you?' his mum yelled from the kitchen. 'It 'asn't got wedged for weeks with all this dry weather. And I've got an 'eadache.'

'Here's your coffee. I had to go all the way to the Co-op for it.' Caleb swung the plastic carrier bag onto the table with a dull thunk.

'Watch it!' She slid her arm across the chipped Formica top, grabbed the jar and heaved herself from her slump and over to the kettle. 'Have you got me change?'

Caleb slammed down the coins and headed to his bedroom. He'd another two hours to wait before he met Lilith again. He took the stairs two at a time and whacked his door back against the wall too.

'Caleb!' His mum screeched from downstairs.

'Hello.'

Caleb didn't even flinch. 'You're early and in the wrong place.'

'I'm bored and I have a plan.' Lilith patted the bed beside her. 'It's time to move to something bigger.'

Caleb stayed standing. 'The papers are full of it all. David only just got out in time.'

Lilith stood too, close up. She smelt of the damp bank of a wooded stream, alive and green. 'You said you wanted them to fear you, to pay attention to you. Well they're doing that now.' Her eyes, on the same level, didn't even flicker as he locked stares. Caleb closed his, to break the circuit. He took a deep breath, her smell; he forgot the words on his lips only seconds earlier. Her fingers scraped through his hair from his temple to bunch in the longer curls at the back and he opened his eyes wide, taking in a shuddering gulp of air.

'This one last task will take you into your full power.' She swayed a fraction closer. 'Then you'll be able to have whatever you want.'

'Caleb, you stupid bugger.' His mother's voice accompanied her unsteady footsteps up the stairs. 'What have you been up to?' Lilith disappeared seconds before his bedroom door slammed into the wall a second time.

'What?'

'There's a picture that looks like you on the telly. Some bloke says you've been starting fires up on the hills. They want to talk to you in connection with the other fires.'

'It's not me.' Caleb's stomach leapt like he'd gone over the crest of a hill on the bus. 'I haven't been up on the hills. I spend all me time at Shaun's. Ask him.'

'Well if it's not you, you've got a twin somewhere. The neighbours'll be on to you in…' She stared at him. 'Jesus; David at number seven. Why'd you do that to him, poor harmless sod?'

'He's not fucking harmless.' Caleb saw the flecks of spit flying across to spatter his mum's face. 'He's a fucking paedo. Do you know what his price was for a cup of sugar? Huh? It was a hand job. But you wouldn't know that would you, 'cos you never went and asked him for it, did you?' Caleb grabbed his hooded jacket and pushed past his mum where she swayed, grey-faced, hands against the wall like an illegal immigrant caught in a spotlight.

****

Lilith manipulated the layers of time and space so Caleb left his house unseen. She wanted things a little messier before she let the full weight of destruction land on him. Once he was in too deep.

She waited to be certain he headed for their glade before leaving him to make his own way there, then she slid between dimensions. It was easier than walking.

Half an hour later, Caleb slipped between the trees to join her and glanced around as if expecting others to be there. 'This isn't a safe place anymore. That bloke with the cap will have told the police about it.' He brushed his hand over the surface of the moss wrapped around the tree trunk and Lilith saw the tension in his face soften.

'Don't worry about that.' She watched as he eased himself to the ground with a sigh. 'This place is unavailable to them. Now that you've learned to work with the life force at a basic level, it allows you to step into the interstices where they can't follow.'

'I love this place.' His energy settled into the rhythm of the glade.

Lilith brushed away his emotion from her thoughts. 'Well it's your base for now. It doesn't sound as if you can go back.' How does it feel to be homeless? To have your life destroyed around you, human?

'Ask me if I care.' Caleb stretched out among the grasses and buttercups. 'What's this last task you want me to do?' She watched as he moved up close to one flower head.

'The Hexagon Centre; I want you to destroy the shopping centre.'

'Why?' He brought his fingers up to and through the light-filled life force surrounding the bloom.

Lilith dragged her eyes from his caresses. 'Because their buying, buying, buying is at the heart of the destruction of the natural world.' The whorl at the centre of her being flashed energy. Caleb would have called it fury.

'Fair enough, but it'll have to be at night.' He stuck the tip of his nose into the life force of the flower and smiled.

'Why?' Lilith knew he would feel the effervescence there. No! No human would truly understand the depth, the connection.

'So I don't get caught and no-one gets killed.' He turned his blue eyes on her. The life force shimmered there too. 'I'm not a murderer.'

All humans are.

****

Sitting deep within the regimented shrubs, Caleb watched for The Hexagon security patrols. He'd already checked out cameras during the day and found what he thought was a blind spot at the corner between the delivery yard and the new Marks and Spencer's.

'I'll set up a fire at four different points; right at the centre and at the end of each of the three arms of the place.' He spoke aloud. Even though Lilith wasn't physically present, her energy brushed against him, raising the hairs from the nape of his neck to the base of his spine.

He closed his eyes, followed the flow of his breath through the eye of the needle of the present moment; now, now and now. The path through the vortices, like a faint trail in the dewy grass, grew clearer with each passage. Everything existed in energy format at this level. Everything. Caleb sensed Möbius strips of other levels, dimensions beyond, but he couldn't break through the elastic, resistant barrier between. He had tried.

He drew his focus laser-tight then split it four ways to the areas bursting with incendiary motion — fabrics, cooking fats, alcohol — and used energy of his own to excite the minute whirlwinds further. Unnoticed, unbidden, he rose to his feet and walked beyond the shrubs.

'There he is; I told you the infrared had picked something up.' The words pressed at the edges of Caleb's awareness. Shadowy figures hovered, human-shaped, about the spirals within spirals. Deep in the shopping centre the flames crackled and leapt in their chosen places; he could withdraw.

He pinged back into himself like a released elastic band, but not so far as to break through into the everyday world. The human shadows before him separated and edged towards him.

'Stop where you are. The police are on their way.' A male voice, deep and rough like sandpaper.

Caleb pushed against the barrier between dimensions, trying to escape.

'He looks stoned to me.' Female, nervous.

'What's your name?'

Nothing gave; Caleb's energy-form bounced back.

'Shit! He's the one they're looking for, the arsonist.'

There had to be a way.

Sirens in the distance. 'They're coming, son. Put your hands on your head, come quiet…'

He wondered… if he *followed* the strip…

Alarms blasted out all around them.

'Christ, what's that?' The man.

…would he end up on the *inside* of the dimension? Caleb played with the strands.

'Fire! Crap, he's done it again, look at the smoke.' The woman.

There. From one dimension to another. That's how Lilith does it.

'Where did he g—' The deep voice was sliced to silence.

Where was he?

Caleb existed between dimensions, in a grey void he had never been to before.

****

Lilith paced the little glade. Even in the absence of men her hips rolled and swayed, figure-of-eighting through the sunbeams and darting insects.

He'd broken through. He shouldn't have been able to. She hadn't shown him that. She plumped down on the mossy tree trunk.

Where is he? He should be back by now. Is he lost? A ripple of fear ran through her body. Between dimensions?

She couldn't leave him *there*; he didn't know the way out. Her soul would be forfeit too if she abandoned him to the grey void. She was responsible for this mess.

Lilith imagined she could see the pattern of flattened buttercups in the grass where Caleb had lain two days before. It drew her as if he held out his arms to her, as a lover. She slid off the tree and into the indentation.

And if he wasn't lost, she'd created a human with devastating powers; able to destroy all around him. Lilith eased her body full length into his imprint. She'd follow his trail.

And if she found him she might have to kill him. A deep ache she'd never felt before bloomed behind her ribs.

****

A familiar buzz intruded on the vast, cold darkness. He turned towards it.

Was he a *he*?

Could he turn?

What was his purpose?

To be. To live.

He sped toward the vibration.

'Caleb.' A soft voice.

Caleb? Was that him?

A pathway like a snail trail glittered ahead of him. He followed.

Caleb opened his eyes to an indigo sky sparkling with stars, fringed by ink-black flutterings.

Leaves.

'Caleb?' A woman's voice; one he knew.

He pushed up onto his elbows and her face came into view, lit by flames. 'Lilith.'

'You're back. I called you back.' He heard a tremor there.

'I know. Thank you.' Caleb reached out to let the little moss fronds dance on his fingertips, cool and soft. The life force of the tree trunk caressed him, welcomed him home.

'I have a final task for you.' Lilith eased herself down beside him so that they touched at shoulder, elbow, hip and ankle. 'The old woods, in the valley bottom, you have to destroy them; burn them.'

He watched her energy spiral, tight and potent. He saw readiness on her face. He felt fear. She's testing me. *Why?* 'Why?'

'So the humans will be afraid of you. So they will take notice of you.' She watched him back, it seemed.

She's afraid of… me.

In his core resided a flicker of the vast, cold darkness. Nothing will ever fill the void. The void is unfillable. 'No, I won't destroy the old woods. I won't destroy anything again.' He raised his eyes to hers.

Lilith offered her hand, her face clear and smiling, her energy wild and dancing. 'I have a better job for you: come help protect them.'

He took it.

THE FLAME

GARY BONN

I'VE TESTED THE SOUND EQUIPMENT and dimmed the lights in the hall. People flood in, holding hands, wishing they were holding hands, or glad that they are not.

And you glide like a shark entering a lagoon full of fish.

You fascinate, you scare me. Sweaty palms, holding my breath, tearing my gaze away so you don't see me looking.

For everyone else, you radiate throughout the hall. Boys swell their chests, girls fawn. Everyone looks at you.

Oh beautiful, oh clever, oh stunning… *you.*

Yes, you're bright. Ok then, the brightest. You know that I have to work twice as hard as you to stay at the top. Is that what this is about? You want to break me so you can always be first at everything?

The funniest jokes, wittiest observations come from you. But you're more evil than anyone I know.

You're quick. A sprinter, a fencer, your foil and sabre hit me more than mine reach you.

You're hot, and *don't you know it.* Is there a single male — pupil or teacher — in this school that doesn't want you? And dream about you in quiet, private moments? Has there ever been a man who passed you in the street and wasn't transfixed?

You pull me in, quicken my pulse. When you're close I'm high, dizzy, flying. The dazzling smiles, the tossing your hair and swinging your hips at me when we all practised for this ceilidh.

You know that's my weak spot — when you're close. That's what you're good at, finding weakness. Do you actually *hate* boys? Or fear them? Why are you so cruel to them?

And why are you after me? Is this game all about proving that you can snare a guy that other girls want — and then discard him?

How many of your old flames have you crucified? Mike… oh, he was so popular with you when his band got a support contract. But all that hanging on his arm stopped when the deal fell through.

Jack… your interest in him shrank with his bank account. Did you keep him hungry until he gave you the next present? Was it all warmth and praise when he pressed the gift into your hands, his grateful puppy eyes begging for an approving smile? Perhaps he got a kiss on good days.

I can't make you out. I have no band deals or bank account. Is it only my resistance that makes you do all the lingering eye contact?

Why am I even thinking about you still? Get out of my head.

Here we go then, Christmas dance. All the girls look stunning. The boys are a blaze of tartans and swinging kilts. Everyone smiles — we can't help ourselves. There's Nathan with his bagpipes, his quick grin and beer on his breath.

We're all going to have fun. At a ceilidh, the biggest social event of the year.

There's Aylidh, all curls, smiles and hanging round in front of me. There's a look in her eye, friendly, open and honest. She's nowhere near as attractive as you. But she doesn't dig her way into your mind and smoulder. Her smile says, ' like you. I hope you like me too.' Any bloke with sense would go for her.

But I'm going for no one. I need three As. I need them like I need oxygen. No time for girls. It's like living in a vacuum.

And I'm not going for *you*. Everyone thinks I'm your next victim. This is your moment. You can get into my space, but I won't give in.

If I did, it would only amount to a kiss in public. I'd be all over you, unable to help myself, and you'd just love it. A kiss of triumph in front of an audience, your victory exhibited all around you: 'Ha! I can have anyone I want.'

Through the Dashing White Sergeant, Strip the Willow, The Gay Gordons, you get too close every time we touch and pass. Your scent throws me again and again. I catch my breath, full of your perfume. Our arms lock, elbow to elbow: I'm weightless. Your hair in my face, soft, intoxicating. You fall against me and laugh, face pressed against my neck. Hand on my cheek. In front of everyone.

Mantis.

Eat my heart, suck the life from me, like you did with all the others; leave me for dead.

There it is, that look from you. 'How close am I now? Can he resist anymore? Have I won?'

The last dance stops, people laughing and hugging each other. You're keeping an arm round my waist, leading me over to your table. You pull yourself against me — but like I'm doing it. All your friends there watching. I'm on display. I feel drunk and my tongue won't work. So close to you I can hardly breathe.

Your thigh, your side, your breasts through the thin silk. Hot.

Elation, fear... too many feelings raging inside me; I don't know what I feel any more.

How can you take control of me like this? You're on fire, scorching. I'm a moth in a flame.

From Seed

Shuna Meade

THE PACKET OF SEEDS the fortune-teller had thrust into Simon's reluctant hands lay on the kitchen table.

'What are these?' Sally asked, shaking the brown packet. 'Oooh, drugs? You are a dark horse, Simon Muckley.' She gave him one of those looks that told him she knew exactly what she was talking about. Sally might look sweet and innocent but, like a Catholic schoolgirl fantasy, she wasn't.

Simon snatched them back. 'Do you always have to think the worst? They're seeds for the garden. I told you what Morag said: I'm to grow a garden. These are my starter seeds.'

Sally snorted. 'You can't even grow grass… I mean, look at the place.' She waved a manicured hand toward the kitchen window and the scrubland beyond.

There used to be a garden there, in his grandfather's time. The old man had a magical touch with plants and when he died, the garden seemed to wither and die with him. Simon's parents paved the area once he'd grown and left home, leaving a border for shrubs, preferring ease of upkeep. When Simon inherited the house, he'd pulled up the paving stones, dug over the plot, brought in new topsoil and planted grass seed. He could have bought sod, 'ready-made grass' Grandpa Pete used to call it, laughing at the concept. 'If you're going to plant grass, start from scratch. It's all about the seeds, my boy.'

Simon's seeds lay dormant. Six month later when nothing grew, he tried a vegetable patch of carrots and radishes, but the tiny green shoots barely broke the surface of the earth before they too shrivelled.

Grandpa Pete's garden flourished, so why not now? Where was the life? If green fingers existed, Simon figured he hadn't inherited them.

FROM SEED

Even the pot plant his mum gave them as a housewarming present died within a couple of weeks.

They'd been so excited about having a house of their own when they'd first moved in. Simon's mum had moved into a smaller flat closer to the centre of town where all her friends were. She found a new lease on life with the move. Simon had never seen her happier.

Things hadn't gone quite so well for Simon and Sally. They argued a lot. Sally wanted kids straight away and Simon wanted time with her, alone, for a couple of years at least. The three-bedroom house with the garden was a perfect way to start a life together but, as the months passed and no babies came, Sally said those extra bedrooms mocked her. And when Simon found he couldn't perform, she'd withdrawn from him, throwing herself into work.

Sally worked part-time, in a music shop. It's how they'd first met. Simon had wanted a new harmonica and she'd been there to sell him the best they had. She played the acoustic guitar and soon they began to jam together; music became their glue.

Her passion for life had dwindled recently, strangely in parallel with his own… Now she watched too much day-time TV, and drank too much coffee with his mother. Simon knew he should be pleased they got on so well, but couldn't shake the feeling his mother's motives included encouraging grandchildren.

Simon looked out at the barren garden and shrugged his thin shoulders, trying to appear nonchalant, uncaring. In truth, Sally's barbs hurt. What had gone so wrong between them? When they'd first married, living in the cramped little flat over the grocery shop, they'd laughed about their meagre existence, they'd made plans for their future, they'd been happy… hadn't they? Ever since they'd moved into the house, things had changed. The swell of anger and frustration expanded in Simon's chest, leaving no room for air. He felt suffocated.

That's why he'd had his palm read. Something needed to change. The flier came through their door last week: *Stuck in a rut? Need a new direction? Let me give you a helping hand. Palm readings by appointment.* He'd chucked it away but dug it out of the overflowing rubbish bin in the sitting room yesterday.

****

Morag wasn't surprised to see him. 'Come on in, Simon, take a seat,' she said from her chair. There was no weirdness, no uncomfortable silence or, worse, prying questions. He had questions about her, but they could wait. She looked good, though. Almost twenty years had passed since they'd last seen each other and in that time she'd matured into a striking woman, but something remained of the girl he'd played with and fallen in first-love with. The same thick dark hair cascaded over her shoulders, her smile wide and infectious, and her skin radiant.

Simon felt himself relaxing in the soft armchair pulled close to the table. The matching red velvet curtains which hung across the only window gave the 'reading room' a warm, womb-like feel. No natural light filtered into this inner sanctuary.

He held out his right hand when she asked, and fought the urge to lift it to her cheek the moment her cool skin touched his, afraid of the emotions that had reawakened.

'What is it you seek?' she asked, eyebrows raised like arches. The directness of her stare, devoid of judgement, didn't make him glance away, the way Sally's did. He felt a sudden pang of regret that their friendship had died, snuffed out by the fire that fateful night.

Momentarily lost in memories, Simon's attention snapped back to the present. What did she ask? *What is it you seek?*

Life. A new life, he wanted to say, but that was too flippant. Why else would he be here if he didn't want to make some kind of drastic change? 'I want to grow — ' he blurted out but didn't finish the sentence. What did he want? He tried again. 'To find my place in this world… to find the thing I am meant to be, meant to do. I'm at a crossroads. All I know is, I can't keep doing what I'm doing now. I need to make a change, but I don't know what that is…' He stopped himself from babbling. She made him feel so comfortable he was unafraid to admit the truth.

Morag nodded and stared again at his palm. She traced the life, head, and heart lines with slender fingers unadorned by rings. He felt a tingle as she brushed over his simple wedding band.

Morag leaned across the table and smiled. 'You will live a long and fulfilling life,' she said. 'You will find joy in creating and nurturing, working with your hands.' She paused for a moment. 'Simon, the answers you seek are in your garden.' He wanted to roll his eyes but thought better of it. 'I remember your Grandpa Pete — he had the magic touch. You have it too, Simon.'

He looked at her, surprised she should even mention his granddad. It had been such a long time ago. He shook his head.

'You do,' she insisted. 'I remember the way you played the harmonica in the garden. The plants responded to the music that came from inside you. You made it possible for me to dance. Plant these seeds and play the harmonica to them.'

'But everything I plant dies.'

'The environment is too toxic — it needs the joy of music to flourish. The seeds will grow. Trust me. I know you believe in me, you always did. Now you have to learn to believe in yourself.'

When Morag gave him the packet of seeds, with instructions to plant them at noon the next day, he'd been disappointed — he wanted answers, not flowers that wouldn't grow anyway. He tried to give them back, but she insisted he take them.

****

The sun woke Simon the next morning. He lay beside Sally, luxuriating in Sunday morning laziness, until he remembered the seeds. How strange that a packet of innocuous seeds had caused a sense of subconscious excitement. The clock on the bedside table read 06:32. He never woke this early, even on a workday. He listened to Sally's shallow, rhythmical breathing. She'd sleep until nine or ten if he was lucky.

Simon slipped from the vastness of the king-sized bed and padded into the bathroom, closing the door. He stared at himself in the mirror. His ears stuck out too far, making his long, thin face look like a pencil with wings.

Sandy brown hair receding, like his dad's and Grandpa Pete's. Damn those genes. He leaned on the ceramic sink and peered at his hairline. His dad lost most of his hair at thirty-seven and Simon sighed at the inevitability. He kept it short and neat and inspected the comb each morning, counting the number of hairs he'd lost. Women didn't like balding men. The day was fast approaching when he'd shave it all off — total baldness in preference to partial baldness. He didn't share these concerns with Sally, though. She'd make him use the hair tonics and special shampoos advertised on TV. Simon smiled ruefully. Advertising was his business.

A successful advertising campaign raised an issue you didn't realize you should be concerned about, and made you concerned. Then it promised a solution. Buy this product and you won't ever need to worry whether the person behind you can see your bald patch. Yeah, right. The only way to prevent that was to wear a hat.

Do you sneeze too often? Are the germs lurking behind your toilet making your family sick? Do you wonder if the stench at the gym is you? Whatever an advertiser could get you to worry about, they would.

Simon had always worked in advertising but had grown cynical of late; he'd lost the will to find creative ways to sell products he didn't believe in. Passionless campaigns, like his life. Had Morag been able to tell that about him?

He saw the shambling reflection of his morning self and admitted his life sucked. Thirty-four years old, losing his hair, married to a woman he felt distanced from, and bored with his job. Great. He needed to make some changes or he'd turn into his father, a bitter old man with a temper and too many resentments. No wonder his mum divorced his father.

What had Morag said yesterday? He'd have a fulfilling life? Simon stared at his reflection, toothpaste now foaming around his lips as he brushed. He spat the suds into the basin.

Fulfilled?

Fulfilled wasn't the word that sprang to mind when he assessed his current situation. How had he let things get to this state? Time to re-evaluate. Action always made him feel better, as if he'd re-taken control.

Simon dressed and hurried downstairs to the kitchen. The remains of last night's Indian takeaway still strewn on the counter top, the smell permeating the downstairs as if it had seeped into the walls, carpets, and curtains by osmosis. The yellow stain of korma smeared on plates, mounds of hardened rice grains like hamster droppings, the once fragrant sauce now congealed in tinfoil containers. Simon swept the whole lot into a black bin bag and unlocked the back door. The coolness of the early morning air bit his skin, making it tighten so the downy hairs on his arms stood to attention.

The morning sun cast long shadows across the plot and he remembered a time as a child, seeing the garden stuffed with flowers, blossoming under Grandpa Pete's care. He remembered how much joy his granddad got from it. How he'd spent hours tending his plants.

How he and Morag had played together as children. Then, as young teenagers, how he'd played the harmonica and she'd danced for him around the statue of Venus that used to stand in the centre of the lawn.

With new eyes, Simon looked at the patch of 'garden' that lay like an empty brown canvas, and he began to wonder. To be able to create something beautiful, something for him, something that didn't need to sell an idea or a product, something to be enjoyed peacefully through all the senses... Was it even possible for him? *Be open to new ideas*, he reminded himself. Something needed to change. He felt an urge to get on with the planting right now but Morag's instructions played over in his head: *Plant the seeds at noon.*

Seeds. Where were those seeds? Simon hurried inside, scanned the kitchen, unable to remember where he'd put them. Think, think, think. Somewhere safe...

He spotted the small brown envelope on the windowsill, tore at the flap and tipped the contents into his palm. Six seeds, nothing more. Tipping them back into the envelope, he folded the top over twice, slipped it into his back pocket for safekeeping and wandered outside.

A memory surfaced. That night... that night, when the fire destroyed Morag's house next door. Rumours spread that somehow she'd started it. Her mother was a known mystic, reading auras and palms, crystals and tarot cards. She made a living and wanted her daughter to follow, but Morag hadn't been interested in any of that. Psychic or not, she loved to dance. Simon would play the harmonica and she would dance for him, her willowy body so lithe. Even at the age of twelve, she had a natural grace. He would play for hours, until the sun set and she had to go home.

He remembered how someone swore they saw a girl dancing in the garden that fateful night, saw flames engulf her... And yet she was the only survivor, not a burn, blister or a scratch on her. That's when the name-calling had started: Morag the fire-starter, the witch, mad Morag. But Simon knew none of those names were true. She was his friend, and when she'd been shipped off to a foster family fifty miles away, he'd been devastated. His Muse was gone and with it the harmonica playing.

****

Simon didn't know how long he'd been standing there when he heard a tapping on glass. He turned and looked toward the house. Sally beckoned from the upstairs bedroom window. He left the garden and trudged to their bedroom.

'Come and make love to me, Mr Muckley,' she said in the child-like voice that used to turn him on. She held her arms out to him and, when he sat beside her on the bed, he noticed she'd put on perfume and changed her long cotton nightdress for a new negligee.

She tugged at his jeans, undoing the top button, lowering the zipper in one swift movement and pulling his boxers around his ankles. 'Take me now,' she whispered in his ear. Hot minty breath filled the air between them as he lay beside her. She pulled him on top of her, spreading her legs to make it easy for him and began to gyrate her pelvis. Nothing happened. Simon didn't rise to the occasion. 'What is it?' she asked, almost tenderly.

He rolled onto his side and sat up. 'I can't do this right now.'

In an instant, Sally's face crumpled. 'What's wrong? Is it me? What's happened to us, Simon?

'I'm sorry. I'm… I've got to go.' He rolled out of bed and pulled on his clothes. He needed to take a walk, to think, to clear his head.

****

When Simon returned to the house at quarter to twelve he stood, surprised to see his mother's car in the driveway. She never visited on Sundays. The moment he pushed open the front door, he knew he'd rather be anywhere else.

The two women sat at the kitchen table, a half-empty packet of chocolate digestives, and another of choc-chip cookies between them. Coffee cups filled, steam still rising. Sally's eyes turned to him then away, all puffy and red-rimmed.

'Hey, Mum.' He bent to kiss his mother but she turned her cheek. 'Steady on girls, a chocolate binge, eh?' He made his voice light, teasing, but neither woman looked at him.

'I'll be in the garden.' He hurried to the back door, relieved there hadn't been a scene. He'd interrupted a 'girls' session', as Sally liked to call the confidential tête-à-têtes she enjoyed with her girlfriends. That now included his mother. He knew without asking what the topic of their conversation had been, and he wanted no part of it.

The door of the garden shed stood wide open. Simon frowned. The rusty padlock dangled and the contents of the shed lay strewn across the floor as if someone had been searching for something. Sally's handiwork? He didn't have time to worry about it.

He found a trowel and a watering can, which he filled from the garden tap at the side of the house, and checked his watch. 11.55am. Morag had told him to plant one seed in each corner of the garden and two in the centre. He dug a small hole six inches deep in each place and stood with hands on hips waiting for the alarm on his watch to go off. Were Morag's instructions precise to the minute? It did no harm to wait for the appointed time.

Beep, beep, beep. The alarm made him jump. He pulled the seed packet from his back pocket, unfolded it, and tipped the seeds into his cupped hand. With great care, he dropped a single brown seed into each little hole before returning and covering them over with the soil he'd piled alongside. He took the watering can and doused each spot. He returned to the shed and found six white plastic markers, which he stuck into the ground beside each patch of darkened earth. OK, what now? He'd water them each morning before heading to work; that way he wouldn't forget.

He didn't want to return to the inevitable problems inside so he set about tidying the shed. Grandpa Pete's tools showed their age: an old-fashioned manual lawnmower, rusted but salvageable, stood against the back wall; a garden hose, coiled like a green snake and mottled with a layer of brown dust. He found gloves and a couple of old broad-brimmed hats, which he stowed on nails on the walls. He pottered around, rearranging and sorting through the tools, flower pots, seed trays, netting, and bamboo stakes. Then he found it, his old harmonica, still in its box! Had Grandpa Pete kept it for him, all this time? He rubbed at the specks of rust and put it to his lips. As he played, the long forgotten sound spilled from it, notes blending and blurring. He wandered out to the garden and walked the perimeter, playing music he barely remembered. If the seeds did grow, he had everything he needed to tend to them, including the harmonica.

Simon didn't know for sure what seeds nestled in the ground. They could be vegetables, or flowers, they could be grass seeds, or some exotic plants. He didn't have a clue, but he would play for them with his childhood harmonica, just as Morag had instructed.

Several hours had passed by the time he stamped into the kitchen, shaking the dirt and mud from his shoes. He grabbed a beer from the fridge and slumped in front of the TV in the sitting room. He flicked the remote from Sally's soap opera channel until he found the football match, put his feet up, and took a long slug of the beer.

Voices floated from the bedroom. He heard footsteps on the stairs and the front door slam. He glanced out the window in time to see his mum climbing into the car, while Sally loaded a suitcase into the back seat. What the — ? Simon didn't move from his chair. At least Sally was with his mum, not off with another man. Did he even care? He realised he didn't.

****

Simon woke before the alarm, with a fluttering of Christmas-morning excitement not experienced since boyhood. He stumbled to the window and looked down at the garden. He rubbed the sleep from his eyes and looked again. Nothing.

He showered and donned his business suit before heading downstairs. With a cup of coffee in hand, he ambled out into the garden. The white markers stood like stakes and he used them to direct the flow of water from the watering can. 'Come on little plants, let's see you.'

His day dragged by, an endless round of meetings, emails, phone calls, more meetings, listening to pitches from junior account managers. Simon found he couldn't concentrate for more than a few minutes at a time and left early, telling his secretary he needed to see the dentist.

He didn't bother going through the front door. Instead, he unlatched the side gate and headed into the garden. What he saw astonished him. In each corner, green sprouts poked above the brown earth. The two seeds in the centre had grown into yellow flowers and Simon crouched, reaching out with tentative fingers to feel their silky petals. He grinned. See, he could make something grow.

He hurried inside to tell Sally but the house stood silent, empty.

FROM SEED

He changed out of his suit and began to think about dinner. When Sally hadn't returned by six o'clock, he called her mobile, which went straight to voicemail. He tried his mother. The phone rang and rang. He called Sally's mobile again and left a message: 'Just wondering what you want to do for dinner. I'm heading to Waitrose in ten minutes so give me a call if there's anything in particular you want.'

He ate dinner alone that night… and slept sprawled across the centre of the bed.

As morning light streamed through the open curtains, Simon rolled out of bed and hurried to the window. He raced downstairs and out the back door without bothering to dress. He could see tiny shoots of grass pushing through the earth where none had taken root before. In each corner, full, lush bushes now grew. In the centre of the plot, more flowers sprouted, pinks, purples, yellows, oranges. Simon spent half an hour watering every plant and he played the harmonica for them. He was late for work.

When he returned home that night, he went straight to the garden. The sight of so much life, so much colour, made him smile. He spent the evening with a gardening book he'd bought on his way back from work.

Sally didn't return that night. When he called the mobile, it went to voicemail and his mother's phone rang and rang. Simon went to bed early and fell asleep with the gardening book open beside him.

He woke even earlier the next morning. Outside in pyjamas and bare feet, he walked on dew-wet grass, now long enough to need mowing. More plants and flowers had grown over night. The once barren plot was now a mature garden, bursting with life. Simon used the hose to water his garden. This time more melodies blew from his lips, through the little instrument. It took longer than he'd anticipated to water everything and by the time he finished, he was late for work, again.

When he returned home that evening, the sight of an overgrown garden made him laugh out loud. Whatever those seeds were, something magical had happened. He hurried inside, changed into an old pair of jeans, now designated as gardening clothes, and set to work. He pulled the rusted lawnmower from the shed and pushed it back and forth. He dumped the grass cuttings behind the shed, a compost heap, just as he remembered from Grandpa Pete's time. Again he played, embracing the beauty of the sounds he made.

He fell into an exhausted sleep that night, still in his gardening clothes, and when he woke at the break of dawn, he tumbled out of bed and down to the garden. He stared at the jungle of vegetation.

Simon didn't go to the office that day — he had too much work to do in his garden. He mowed the lawn, weeded, cut back the bushes, chopped and pruned, cleared and watered. And, by the time darkness fell, he climbed into bed, exhausted again and still clutching the harmonica.

Something woke him at 3am. He staggered to the window. The light of the moon shone upon his beautiful garden. Simon stared. A woman danced around the central flower bed, joyful, arms and hands reaching skyward, a fluidity to her movements. Morag? He reached for the harmonica and music poured from his window. He watched as she swayed and leaped, pirouetted and reached, with a mesmerising litheness, long hair streaming behind her. Simon couldn't tear his eyes away. The quickness of steps made it look as if she danced with a weightless body.

As he watched, she whirled, like a dervish, the music faster now, a blur of flowing hair and fabric, faster and faster until she burst into a fireball so bright Simon shielded his eyes. When he looked again, the woman had vanished.

Simon slept late. On waking, bleary-eyed and with an aching body, he rolled out of bed and stumbled into the bathroom. His dreams troubled by images of a woman dancing in the garden, colours swirling about her, moonlight, flames, music, darkness. He splashed water on his face and when he looked in the mirror, he struggled to recognise what stared back at him. Exhaustion etched the canvas of his face, deepening the creases, but he couldn't deny the sparkle in his eyes. He had to get down to his garden.

More flowers had sprung to life overnight. Roses in shades of pink and red entwined along the fence, lupines thrust skyward, pansies, primroses, and forget-me-nots nestled in the rock garden he'd created. Giant daisies, geraniums, flowering shrubs, and rhododendrons grew along the borders. He knew all their names — he'd studied hard, and tended them with gentleness. The buds of new life surrounded him and he rejoiced in the beauty of his garden. 'I made this garden,' he shouted to no-one, but the voicing of it filled him with pride.

He wanted to share his exhilaration with Sally. He wanted to show her what he'd created. He realised that he missed her. Where was she? How long had she been away? Days? Weeks? Time blurred, merged, like the notes of the harmonica. He didn't know the day or the date.

He called his mother. This time she answered. 'Mum? Where's Sally?' Without waiting for an answer, he continued on, unable to hold back his joyful enthusiasm. 'I've got something incredible to show her, to tell her. Something amaz—'

His mother interrupted, 'Simon! Simon, hold on a minute. What's wrong with you? She left you six months ago.'

Simon crumpled to the floor, the phone still clutched to his ear.

****

The day Sally returned home, Simon filled the house with flowers cut from his garden, the air heavy with sweet scents. Posies of sweet peas crowded the kitchen windowsill, every surface adorned with flowers, so bright, so vibrant that the moment she walked in, her eyes filled with tears, her smile wide and genuine.

'I grew these for you, Sally,' he said, pointing to the red roses in the centre of the table. 'I've made a few changes to my life. I left my job and I'm working on the garden full-time now. I'm supplying flowers to the Country House Hotel in Kingsbridge and they pay top rates. Turns out I have green fingers after all. I just needed a helping hand to get me started.'

When he led her into the garden, her mouth dropped open at the lushness of the plants. He took out his harmonica and played for her, his tongue playing across the holes, breath blowing and drawing. He bent the notes, tongue moving, mouth shaping, moulding the force of his breath, serenading her the way he did when they first met, with passion and yearning.

After the call with his mother, he'd fought for Sally with passionate love letters. Every day he sent fresh flowers gathered from his garden. He'd courted her all over again until she relented…

He pulled her into his arms and kissed her gently, unsure of her reaction. She didn't pull away. Hand in hand, they walked around the garden. He pointed out every flower, every plant. He felt content, whole. 'I've figured it out,' he told her. 'I've found my calling. Morag was right, she showed me the way. But there's something missing in my life, Sally. You. I love you, I always have.'

Simon looked across at his wife and squeezed her hand. 'There's life in our garden. I think it's time we filled our house with children.'

THE BANYAN CONNECTION

ALF HAYWOOD

'HE'S A LYING, CHEATING, LOATHSOME rat and I hate him, Grangie,' Monique said, burying herself in her grandmother's arms and sobbing uncontrollably.

Grangie held on tight to her youngest and favourite granddaughter, smiling again at the childish nickname she'd been given by Monique so many years earlier. 'It not his fault,' she replied, her eyes full of sympathy as she struggled to remember what it was like to be young and in love. 'He a man, and all men is liars, even your grandpa and he was a good man. His problem was to be too good-looking, and I never did get eyes fitted to de back of me head.'

'What am I going to do, Grangie? I can't go back to work while he's there, telling all sorts of stories about me. How he pretended to love me while he was already cheating with his next conquest.'

'Girl, you gotta go back in dat office and make like he something you trod in dat a dog left in de street. You gotta look down your nose and make him see what he lost: the finest damn girl in de world. When you done dat, when de hurt is gone, den we talk about de future.'

'I don't have a future, Grangie. My whole life is ruined because of him and if I don't go back there I don't know what else I can do.'

'Dat no way to talk! You is wasted in dat office. You got fine bones like me mother, you tall like your grandpa and you have de talents like your mama. We know you is de best to read and write and work in dem offices.'

'I'm not the best and it's a lousy job really but it's all I know. How can I go back there while everyone is laughing at me for being such a stupid fool?'

'Never no mind bout dem. You go back like nuttin happen at all.

You still wear the short skirts to give all de men de hots an' make dem other girls crazy jealous.'

'Maybe you could do that, Grangie, but I'm not as strong as you are. I know I'll just burst into tears the first time anyone says anything about this.'

'You got de strength girl, but you is not connected to your roots. You a lost person without dat connection, and de next man along will treat you de same 'cos you between de Caribbean and dis place. Right now you is in de middle, and dat is no safe place to be.'

Monique wanted sympathy and a shoulder to cry on, not a lecture on how bad her life was. She knew that already, now that the latest boyfriend had turned into a disaster. But Grangie was always right. She really did feel so much better in the office a few days later, when she encountered the cause of her grief trying to date another possible victim.

Monique stopped in front of them for a moment before saying, 'Girl, I'd like to tell you everything good about that guy. Trouble is, there isn't anything worth telling, except he's a really good liar.'

****

That conversation with Grangie was not the most memorable one Monique had with her beloved grandmother. And although she never forgot the good advice, she didn't do anything about making the connection with her roots. Living in a big city like London, there just wasn't time.

The phone call from her mama changed everything. Monique's comfortable world crashed around her when she heard about Grangie's heart attack. The next few days were a nightmare of sitting outside intensive care, crying and comforting each other, waiting for the inevitable while praying non-stop for the impossible.

The impossible never happened. A week later Monique sat listening to her father reading Grangie's list of bequests. She watched heartbroken as Grangie's few pieces of imitation jewelry were accepted by grateful relatives or friends as if they were more precious than the crown jewels. Even the outlandishly bright, plumed hats that she'd worn to church each Sunday were like gifts from on high to the unworthy. Everyone loved Grangie so much, and wanted something as a last reminder of her.

Near the end of the letter, Monique's father glanced tearfully at Monique and hesitated, trying unsuccessfully to control the emotion in his voice.

'*The house to be sold after everyone take what they want, furniture, mirrors, don't make no mind to me. The money from the house to be divided between my children, they do with the money anything they want, but I prefer a big party, like it the day before judgement and nobody go home early. I say one more thing to Monique 'bout me money in the bank. That all belong you girl after me funeral paid for. I tell you exactly how to spend this money. You party and enjoy life. But not here, not in this place. You go home to your roots girl, you feel the sun on your body, hot and life-giving; you feel that sun. You dream under the Banyan tree, and you dance to the music they play 'til your feet be sore. Maybe then you know about life, and how to love and keep a good man. I tell you go home to your roots and new woman you be.*'

No one said anything after that, just sat silent and sorrowful, listening to Monique crying softly. Monique just wished she could exchange her inheritance for a few more words with Grangie.

The next day she tried to explain to her parents why she couldn't go to the Caribbean. 'I can't go there on my own, mama. It's too far, and I've never even been to the seaside on my own. Why not come with me? We could have a wonderful time together!'

'Definitely not, Monique. This was a special gift for you from Grangie and she wanted it just for you. Maybe one of your friends might be interested in going with you, or I could ask at the church to see if anyone is interested in making the trip?'

The thought of going alone scared Monique more than she wanted to admit. She was absolutely delighted when her cousin Ayida rang to say that she'd been dying to go there for a holiday.

'Monique, it will be amazing. Hot sun, golden beaches, a warm sea to swim in, and dozens of gorgeous guys to take us out dancing every night!'

Ayida's infectious enthusiasm changed everything and over the next few weeks the girls spent a lot of time planning all the wonderful things they intended doing together. The things they wanted to do, the sights they wanted to see and especially the 'gorgeous guys' they hoped to meet.

Just a week before their flight, when their excitement was almost at boiling point, Monique had a disturbing dream. Not only did it frighten her, she also found it difficult to remember. She explained as much of it as she could to her mother the next morning over breakfast.

'I'm not sure exactly what happened, but I was looking at a tree, a really big one, and the next thing I remember was that it was dark and there were people around me pushing me forward and I felt frightened. I sensed something bad was going to happen to me but I didn't know what until I saw the fire in front of me.'

'What sort of fire, girl?' her mother asked casually as she carried on cooking the breakfast. 'Like a bonfire, you mean?'

'No, it was flat on the ground. I suppose it might have been a bonfire but all the wood had burnt down and only the glowing embers were left. There was a man standing beside it and he was wearing a big mask so I couldn't see his face. He just stood there pointing at the fire and the others were pushing me towards it. I could feel the heat getting stronger all the time but there were too many people and I couldn't escape.'

'Probably just indigestion, Monique, although you kinda young for that. Or maybe it's excitement about the holiday. You two are going to have a wonderful time, just like I did when I went back there before I met your daddy. It was exactly the same as I'd remembered it, not so much as a single house had changed.'

'That was a long time ago. I bet it's just like being in any other country now. The internet has changed everything, you know.'

'Not everything child. Those Banyan trees been standing for hundreds of years and I think they know a lot more than any old computer. But you don't have to believe your mama; just you wait and see for yourself.'

The day before the flight, Monique's aunt rang to say that Ayida had been injured in a car crash. 'I'm sorry she can't go with you Monique. The doctor said that the journey would be too difficult with a broken ankle. I'm sure you'll be fine on your own. People there are so warm and friendly. It will be the best holiday of your life, I promise.'

The call was followed by a text from Ayida, who was still in the hospital: *Crying non-stop because I'm not with you. Have a great holiday and party like mad for both of us.*

Monique would be going alone after all, although that didn't seem so bad now it was all organised. The problem was the recurring dream, and the masked man who seemed determined to throw her on top of his fire.

****

At Gatwick airport she could almost touch the excitement near the check-in desks as hundreds of families prepared to visit their family homes and relatives in St Kitts. Young and old were anticipating the experience and Monique couldn't help responding to the exhilarating hubbub around her.

It felt like an anti-climax to move through the security area and sip some coffee in one of the bars while she waited for her flight to be called. She sat there quietly watching the other people, and wondering where everyone was going. Well-dressed business men off to make more money buying or selling something. A sad-looking traveller, possibly going to a funeral, sitting at the same table as a rather obvious pair of newlyweds with bright, shiny wedding rings, who looked as if they wanted to start the honeymoon right there on the table.

There was also a good-looking guy having a losing conversation on the phone with his girlfriend, promising to be there that evening when they could sort out all the problems and start again. Monique felt quite sorry for him until she bumped into him again on the aircraft when he claimed the seat beside her. Her sympathy evaporated when she recognised the familiar smile he gave her as his eyes darted all over her body; yet another love rat on the prowl. He seemed totally at ease, complimenting her on the delicious fragrance of her perfume and hair style, anything that would start a conversation.

She reacted instinctively, furious that he could be so callous, and her withering look must have cut into him like a knife because he fell silent at once. All around her, the babble of animated conversations sounded so infectious and that made her feel even more annoyed because she wanted to be a part of those conversations. It was going to be a long, tedious nine hours of flying.

Two hours later she was forced to start talking to him, partly because he was handing her a meal from the stewardess, partly because she was totally bored maintaining the silence. But mostly because he looked genuinely sorry for his earlier failed attempt to win her attention. For an hour or so they spoke a few times, at first rather distant, then a little friendlier after he told her his name was Jean Paul. With renewed confidence he leant a little closer but Monique realised she was letting her defences down and reverted to silence again.

This verbal cat and mouse game ended when a stewardess organised a seat swap for her with a rather stern woman in her sixties. She was dying to see his face when his new companion sat down beside him but she was already far too engrossed talking to the married couple beside her to look round.

The conversation flowed like a torrent for hours until they could talk no more and all three drifted into sleep. Unfortunately the sleep didn't last very long for Monique and she woke, startled and unable to stifle a cry for help. Her dream had changed slightly; the masked man was still there calling her forward, but he seemed to know she was getting closer and he was laughing or gloating as he waved at her and the burning coals.

Monique tearfully tried to explain her dream, hoping for some more sympathy, but the woman's reply didn't help: 'I don't know what's going on inside your head, girl, but good or bad you're going to find out some time soon. Maybe somebody put a curse on your family from the Caribbean and you are going to be a sacrifice.'

'Rubbish, woman,' her husband said at once. 'The girl is frightened enough without you making it worse. You're just excited about the holiday, that's all it is. After a day or two of relaxing in the sun you'll forget all about it.'

By the time the flight ended she had already pushed the dream to the back of her mind and eagerly joined the seething mass of people waiting to leave the aircraft. She struggled through the various immigration areas before meeting the courier who would guide her to the next stage of her journey. When he said they had to wait for one more passenger, Monique's sixth sense guessed who it was going to be.

He turned up a few minutes later struggling with his luggage and an oversized instrument case.

'Keyboard,' he said, answering her unspoken question. 'I hope you enjoyed the rest of the flight. I, er, sort of wondered what happened to you.'

'Oh I met some friends I knew and I stayed with them when the lady in the next seat offered to swap places.'

'Great, I'm glad it wasn't anything I said that caused it,' he said, looking rather confused. She realised too late that the other woman probably gave him a completely different story when she took Monique's seat.

The courier took them on a short car journey from the airport outside the town of Basseterre to the harbour where they were supposed to board a ferryboat to Charlestown, the principle town on the island of Nevis, the final destination for both of them.

While they waited at the harbour, they listened to a growing row between the courier and the ferry operator. As a distraction from the obvious impending bad news, Monique asked Jean Paul why he was going there.

'The earthquake in Haiti. I was asked to do something to raise money to help the reconstruction programme. I happened to be here with my band when it happened. We raised a few thousand by selling some special CDs and now we're back to show the people a DVD of what happened with the money and hopefully raise some more while we're here.'

'Is that to prove you didn't waste it all on expenses?'

'No, we did it for free because they needed our help. This will be a celebration as well. A few other bands are joining in to make it a competition. That way it will be more exciting and newsworthy. We need to add a few more angles to the next CD so that it sells a lot more copies.'

Maybe it was because she felt some need to belittle him, or maybe she didn't believe he could be so charitable with his time. Instead of appreciating his efforts, she replied, 'That's not a bad idea; you get some great publicity on the back of some charity work and a tax-deductible holiday at the same time.'

Jean Paul didn't reply, he just looked ready to explode before walking away to kick a small stone off the jetty into the sea. Minutes later the courier confirmed the boat would not be leaving as there was a problem with the engine. He would take them back to a small hotel and they would have to stay there for the night.

The standard at the hotel he took them to was pretty basic, but there was, at least, running water and a shower in Monique's room, to wash away the stress and strain of the long journey. After the shower and a change into some fresh clothes she felt a lot better. She also felt a little guilty about her harsh criticism of Jean Paul's motives and decided to apologise to him over dinner. She could hear him trying to sing an old Frank Sinatra song called *Monique* through the paper-thin walls and wondered, with a smile, whether it was just a coincidence.

Dinner was served on a small, open veranda and, with only a few wall lights and a myriad of twinkling stars above them, the view seemed even better when the buildings around them were hidden in the darkness.

It was the perfect setting for a romantic evening; a definite tingle went down her spine and all the way to her toes when she saw Jean Paul leaning over the balcony admiring the view and wearing a stylish shirt and a pair of figure-hugging trousers. As she gave him a very approving look, her mind was telling her to stop making a fool of herself. Instead of listening though, she simply breathed in a wisp of his aftershave and hoped the hotel had some decent wine they could share.

For a few minutes the conversation flowed beautifully as Jean Paul explained more about his band and the different music they played, before they ordered their very simple evening meal. Unfortunately, just before it was delivered to their table, his phone rang again, leaving Monique to listen to yet another one-sided conversation.

'I'm sorry, Jacinta, there was a problem with the boat bringing us over... Us? Just another passenger, she's stranded here the same as I am... No, she's not competition. Look, I'm sorry I can't get there tonight to sort everything out, but we'll do it the moment I get there tomorrow... Of course, I'll explain everything... Yes, I said I'll tell you everything about the last one, but that's all history now.'

The conversation ended just in time for him to watch Monique leaving the veranda, carrying her dinner to the privacy of her room.

Hours later, in the middle of the night, he heard her calling out in her sleep. She sounded frightened at first, but then she let out a terrified scream and he banged on the wall to wake her up.

'Monique, are you OK? Monique, answer me!'

'I'm OK, I'm sorry it was just a bad dream, that's all, I'm sorry.'

'You don't sound OK. Do you want to talk for a while or anything?'

'No, I'm fine, please go back to sleep.'

He might have been tired, but he was wide awake now, listening to every sound coming from her room, unsure whether she was simply rolling over in her bed, or quietly pacing the floor. Even when he heard the gentle rhythm of her breathing, he lay wondering what was disturbing her, and whether it was anything like his own fears.

After an embarrassingly quiet breakfast together, the courier arrived to say the engine repairs would be completed in an hour and they would be on their way as soon as possible. Four hours later they left the harbour in a large ferryboat, cutting through the light swell of the sea with just an occasional high bounce when they collided with a larger wave when they reached the open water between the islands.

The boat trip was almost over when Monique tried to reach her luggage on the far side of the boat. She managed the first step easily but as she made the second the boat turned sharply towards its new mooring and she lost her balance completely, ending up sprawled across Jean Paul and held safely in his arms.

'I was hoping this might happen some time,' he said grinning, 'but I didn't think I stood a chance after you left me alone last night.'

This was followed by a cry of pain as she slapped him across the face and yelled, 'Don't you dare say that, you rat! I hope Jacinta tears your eyes out after you tell her what you've been trying to do since we met.'

He sat down, stunned and speechless. By the time he recovered she had left the ferry and was already sitting in the front passenger seat of the minibus taking them to their hotel.

His smiling friend and drummer, Dave, didn't help the situation as he joined him on the jetty. 'You struck out there, JP. I been telling you for years, you don't have a clue how to talk to girls.'

'No one can talk to that girl; she's a freak who changes her mind faster than the wind. C'mon, help me with the luggage and then tell me what the hell is happening.'

When the minibus pulled away, the keyboard was laid out on the middle row of seats with Jean Paul and Dave sitting in the third row.

Dave started the explanation at once. 'It's too late to sign a deal with Jacinta now. Max decided he needed a new singer as well so he has been chasing her to join his band ever since he arrived. He gave her until last night to sign or he said he would withdraw his offer. The kid was too scared she might end up without any deal, so she signed. After all those weeks of negotiating, we end up out here without a singer and Max is walking around as if he has already won the competition.'

'But I told her I would get a visa for her to join us in the UK for a minimum of a year. I'm sick and tired of dealing with women who don't know what they are going to do next. Let's try and get a male singer; we might stand more chance if we do that.'

Only the driver overheard Monique's barely audible mutter, 'Oh shit,' as she shook her head in disbelief.

At the hotel Jean Paul checked in as fast as he could and then left to find Jacinta, hoping to change her mind somehow. He flew past Monique without even noticing she was waiting at one side to apologise for her stupid behaviour. Within moments she was alone and heading slowly to her room, silently asking Grangie why she had dragged her to this miserable place. From the shade of her bedroom she looked out on the bright sunshine and a few children playing in the dust. It looked exactly like the idyllic holiday location she had imagined. Unfortunately she had almost ruined it before it had begun; it was all too much, so she threw herself onto the bed and cried herself to sleep.

When the dream started it was more vivid than it had ever been before. Everything was crystal clear, even the faces of the people standing beside her, goading her forward. She heard their angry voices demanding that she must be burned on the fire, while the masked man watched, laughing. The difference this time was that she was falling onto the fire and she screamed in agony as the red hot coals burned into her skin.

She awoke, petrified, to the sound of her dying scream. Gasping for breath she realised it was only the dream again but she was terrified of being alone or going back to sleep. In absolute despair she ran fully clothed to the shower and let the cooling water gradually calm her down. It took almost an hour but eventually she felt safe enough to strip off her clothes and change into dry ones.

After that she wandered out into the evening sunlight to experience first-hand the beautiful buildings that surrounded the hotel. Despite her attempts to block Jean Paul's words from her mind, she couldn't help trying to imagine what London would look like after an earthquake and wondering what it would cost in time and money to restore. Then she remembered a television programme about World War II and realised that London had had its own earthquake: it was called the Blitz and had taken a decade to recover from.

In the fading light, she returned to the hotel and went into the dining room hoping to see Jean Paul. She sat alone for an hour before ordering her meal and then ate in complete silence. The receptionist happily confirmed that everyone involved in the band competition was in the marquee, setting up equipment and rehearsing.

'Everyone very excited over there ma'am,' the receptionist said. 'It like carnival this evening, everyone listenin' an' dancin' an' singin'. I think for sure we should be there with all dem good lookin' men.'

'No, I think I'll stay here. I'll have a drink in the bar and see them when they get back.'

Monique had often been out drinking with friends, but she'd never been on her own in a bar for three hours, drinking much more than she would have if she had been dancing or talking as well. When Jean Paul and his friends returned, her eyes were glazed and the world was spinning around her.

Despite that, she took a few unsteady steps towards Jean Paul but before she could apologise she slipped and fell. He leapt forward and caught her head just before it crashed against the floor. After giving him a rather silly grin, she mumbled a few incoherent words and passed out.

Jean Paul and Dave carried her up to her room and carefully laid her on the bed. The concerned receptionist had come with them and she slipped off her shoes and pulled the sheet and blanket over her.

Monique slept through breakfast and most of the morning; it was close to midday when Jean Paul saw her standing in the entrance of the marquee looking a little lost and probably still feeling the effects of the night before.

'How are you?' he asked, far too cheerfully.

'Not good, and the noise in here isn't helping but I have to talk to you,' she replied, struggling to concentrate on what was happening around her.

'Well I don't think you're in any condition to shout at me or slap my face again. Let's go outside and talk in the fresh air.'

'I promise no more shouting or anything,' she said reaching for his arm. 'I'm sorry about everything, I got it completely wrong.'

Sitting on the ground in the shade of the marquee she explained and apologised about everything as best she could, from the first phone conversation that she listened to and all the incorrect assumptions she'd made about him and Jacinta.

At the end of the explanation, Jean Paul leant forward to wipe away a tear from her cheek and grinned broadly, saying, 'Apology gratefully accepted. You've no idea how much I wanted to talk to you on the flight out and I really couldn't understand what I was doing wrong to keep upsetting you.'

'That's exactly how I felt but I didn't want to be the one to break up someone else's relationship.'

'Then there's hope for me yet. Look, I have to visit a few of the other towns and villages to promote the competition this afternoon. Why not come with me in the minibus and we can start all over again?'

'That sounds perfect. All I need is a cup of coffee or some water and I'm ready.'

When they returned that evening all the earlier misunderstandings were forgotten; they had shared a wonderful afternoon. But their plans for a quiet dinner together ended when Dave met them at the hotel to break the news that he had been unable to find anybody who could sing well enough to join the band. With just twenty-four hours to go, he wondered if it was time to back out and concede, as they would have no chance without a vocalist.

'I can sing,' Monique said before she could stop herself.

'Why didn't you say that earlier? Do you sing reggae? Calypso?' Dave asked.

'Neither,' she replied looking extremely uncomfortable. 'Perhaps this isn't a good idea. I've never sung with your sort of band and I don't think I can do it now. I shouldn't have said I could. That's another mistake I've made.'

'What sort of songs do you sing? Maybe we can do one of your numbers?' Jean Paul suggested cautiously as he saw the fear in her eyes.

'I don't sing any proper songs. Not hit-parade stuff. I sing in the choir at church, and in another orchestral choir where my mama plays the piano. I sing classical pieces, Mozart, Beethoven, operettas, absolutely nothing like you play. I've listened to Caribbean music but I've never tried to sing it, and definitely not in front of an audience.'

'Then it's about time you did, and we'll decide afterwards whether it's good enough for a permanent job,' Jean Paul said, imploring her with his eyes to say yes.

After the merest nod of her head, dinner was abandoned and they headed for the marquee to start rehearsing. At first it was terrible, as Monique struggled to sing the rhythms. After an hour it was starting to sound better and after another there were definite signs of progress, although she was still struggling hopelessly with the feel of the music. She wanted to carry on, but the different style of singing was making her throat feel a little sore.

Jean Paul recognised the signs at once and called a halt to the practice. 'It's getting late guys, let's head for the bar and do some planning. I don't think we should wear out our new singer.'

'I feel too hot to sit in the bar, I need some more fresh air,' said Monique, reaching for his hand. 'Could we go for a walk or a drive before it gets too late?'

'Of course, whatever you want now we're friends again. How about a drive *and* a walk? I know a place along the road where the trees reach right down to the beach and we can walk along there in the moonlight, if that's OK?'

'That sounds a bit lonely. Will anyone hear me if I scream for help?'

'No, not a soul, but I won't misbehave if you don't, although the place is called Lover's Beach.'

'Then we'll go but we won't go too far,' she answered with a smile, leaving him to decide what she meant.

They drove for twenty minutes and then walked along the beach for about a mile, slowly, steadily, enjoying each other's company more and more, talking about her grandmother and why she'd come out to the Caribbean. They were laughing together about her becoming a new woman, when he asked about her dream.

'You sounded really frightened that first night, and I heard you screaming again here. I wanted to make sure you were OK but after that slap I was afraid you'd react even more.'

Reluctantly at first, she began to tell him the story; he nearly interrupted a few times but grudgingly allowed her to finish it before saying, 'It's weird, that's the same nightmare I've been having for a long time; ever since I first came here three years ago. The only difference is that I'm facing an old witch doctor and she's pushing me towards the fire. You didn't hear me last night but the boys did; I damn near screamed the place down and I don't ever want to be that scared again.'

Neither of them realised that they had stopped walking while they each revealed their dreams; not until they were wrapped in each other's arms and he suggested sitting on the grass beside an old Banyan tree.

'I thought you were going to behave,' she said, leading him towards the tree. 'Standing here for a while might be safer,' she added, thinking they might both be getting a little too excited. It was only as their lips touched that she realised they were falling into the tree.

The dream became reality and she recognised the masked man standing in front of her, beckoning her forwards, encouraging her to come closer. The grasping hands were there as well, reaching out to touch the light cotton wrap that her clothes had transformed into. She recognised all the faces from her dream, but something was different this time. It took a few seconds but finally she realised they weren't threatening her; they were cheering, and all of them were smiling at her. They weren't pushing her forward; they were encouraging and congratulating her. She could also hear some wild calypso music calling her to follow the beat and dance.

She guessed at once who they were. They weren't enemies or friends; they were her family, her ancestors. Great, great grandparents, uncles, aunts and even her beloved Grangie were there smiling and waving at her. The masked man was slowly lifting his mask away. Instead of threatening her, he was reaching out a hand to hold and she ran towards Jean Paul, knowing it was him long before the mask was discarded.

'Will you come with me?' he asked, pointing at the coals. 'If we have to do this, let's do it together.'

'I know we can, it's what we're here for: to walk across the fire with our families watching and helping us.'

THE BANYAN CONNECTION

They stepped out together, one slow faltering step followed by another and then they started laughing as they realised they couldn't feel any pain, just a dull warmth. But the flames weren't harmless. Her cotton wrap and the one around Jean Paul's waist were burning in the heat, even though they couldn't feel it. As the clothes burnt, he reached out and brushed a few charred remnants from her shoulders and stood transfixed by the sight of her naked body beside him.

The music affected her the most; dragging a reluctant response from her, it called her to dance, slowly at first, but faster as the tempo increased until she became a writhing form, almost a blur as every part of her body responded to the frenetic music. Jean Paul stood facing her, watching spellbound as her hips and torso gyrated effortlessly to the music. He stood almost motionless, trapped by the vision before him as she writhed closer and closer. Unable to resist any longer, he picked her up and ran to the far side and into a small grass hut before laying her on the ground. For a few seconds he knelt beside her, brushing his open palm lightly against her face. He waited until she smiled and nodded briefly before leaning closer to kiss her.

In an instant their eyes opened and they realised it had all been a dream. They were lying, fully clothed, in each other's arms under the Banyan tree.

Jean Paul was the first to speak, his face clouded in confusion. 'What happened? Instead of the witch I was so frightened of, you were there. That was so real. Dancing on the fire and afterwards, after the clothes burned we... In the hut we... Where's the hut gone? We were...'

'It was definitely a dream, but oh God what a dream,' she answered, laughing lightly as she eased away from him. 'I never felt so much passion in my soul. That music reached down to my toes and made me dance like I never danced before. I saw and felt everything you did, and oh God did I feel everything, but I don't think we did anything more than dance.'

'How do you know about the music? Two people can't share each other's dreams can they? We were there together but...' he said, unable to believe what had happened and obviously disappointed they still had their clothes on.

He tried to stand but gave a gasp of pain as the sole of one foot touched the ground.

'It's burnt a little,' Monique said after examining it briefly. 'You should have spent more time dancing instead of standing still like a zombie.'

'I was dancing; I know I was dancing with you after the clothes were burnt. Maybe my feet burned after I picked you up?'

'No, your feet never moved. You were dancing with your eyes only, and they were staring at me, watching every move I made.'

Jean Paul relaxed and laughed lightly, her gentle words confirming the truth. 'I couldn't help it; I've never seen anyone so beautiful in my life. I watched for as long as I could and then…'

'Well maybe something happened, but not what you were thinking about. While I was dancing in the fire I could feel the flames reaching into me, flowing in my veins and giving me a power I didn't know was possible.' Monique sighed. 'Grangie was right about touching my roots, I just didn't realise she meant all those relatives. Falling into that old Banyan tree didn't make anything happen, but it lit a fire in me that will burn for the rest of my life.'

'That fire suits you; it's in your eyes. It looks warm and inviting, just like the rest of you in that dream,' he said, leaning forward to kiss her again. 'I don't think anyone could ever put it out, but I'd love to try and cool it down a little.'

'The fire in me gonna take more than just a little loving to cool down.'

'I don't mind that. I'll keep trying for the rest of our lives if you let me?'

'That might work, but if we keep trying and the loving gets better, I think that fire is gonna get even hotter,' she said, stretching one leg over his body to sit across his thighs.

'That sounds even better; could you make that a promise?' he asked tenderly, reaching out for her hips to draw her closer.

Jean Paul watched the smile spreading across her face as she undid a few buttons of her blouse. Lifting her head to the sky she cried out, 'It easy to promise that,' shouting the words up into the leafy branches of the tree above them. She reached her arms high into the air, her fingers stretching out to touch the stars as she called to Grangie in a long, slow Caribbean lilt.

'Grangie — new woman I be.'

Surreal

Gary Bonn

T HIS MUST BE A DREAM. No *really*. How the hell did I get here? Wherever this is.

Woodland, Scots pine I think. The sky is lightening and, if I look to the east, there's a faint pre-dawn glow over the hills.

I'm dressed in trainers, jeans and a denim shirt. No one goes into the wilderness like this — not if they want to live. What's going on? I hug myself. Frosted leaves crackle under my shoes.

I'm cold. I'm hungry. This is not good. I have a penknife, but nothing with which to make a fire. Cutting strips of bark, I chew the bittersweet sap layer and spit out the woody pulp when there's no goodness left.

The vapour of my breath fogs my progress from one tree to another.

The sound of hooves in the soft, needle-strewn forest floor; they only whisper the weight of the horse. More blasts of vapour from behind a thicket. Through gaps I see the skin of a bay, the red of a velvet cloak and a glint of bronze.

The head of a horse and the tip of a spear come into view. The rider appears next, sees me and stops.

I've seen that helmet before, but where? Oh, come on. It's classic.

The horse turns and paces towards me. The rider drops his spear point as he nears, like I'm a threat, but lifts it as he draws close.

'I know you!' he says. 'But from where do you come? You are not of this land or this world.' He slips from the saddle, buries the butt of the spear into the ground, tethers the bay to a branch and turns to me. 'I know you like my own brother, but I've never seen you before.'

I'm shivering and hugging myself.

He says, 'You're cold. I'll light a fire. Do gather some wood. Not from the ground. Choose small twigs caught in the branches; they will be dry.'

The effort of collecting wood warms me a little and I follow his instructions about size and source. He flicks flint and steel over tinder from a pouch. Crackling twigs spit sparks.

I recognise the helmet at last. 'Wenceslas?'

He pulls the helmet off and places it beside the fire. 'That is my name. But who and what are you? I thought you a demon at first, or fey and faerie.' His dark, sharp eyes invade mine. 'You look human and about my age: just a man. You wear the strangest clothes and they smell even stranger. I should be on my guard, but you carry no threat that I can sense. Who are you?'

'I don't know how to answer that — I'm a bit confused. I don't know where I am either. I've seen that helmet before, photos of it. Are you really Wenceslas?'

'Yes. I know not what you mean by photos, but I know that you come from my dreams. There is magic in this meeting. I would that it be good magic.' He blows tinder and twigs, piles more into a cone and points to my handful of wood. 'We need larger fuel if you are to stop shivering. Break dry sticks and bring them hither.'

I snap dead branches from the trees around; fortunately pines provide so many. *Wenceslas*, when was he around? Was that iron-age, the dark ages, or just legend? This feels neither like reality nor dreaming. What *is* going on?

He piles my sticks on the fire and goes to collect more. The sun rises, gilding the tops of trees. Sparks burst up from the fire. One of them singes my shirt; a puff of smoke and a tiny black hole.

'From where do you come, mystical one?' Wenceslas asks.

'Glasgow. Er, Escotia… Hyperborea? I don't know what you call it. The last memory I have is that of walking from my office to put the kettle on.'

'Even your words are mystical. Now I know who you must be.' He pokes the fire and smiles. 'Your coming is not unexpected. Angels heralded your appearance and I will beg you the favour they claimed was in your power to bestow.'

At last the fire warms me, though I'll smell like a barbecue. 'Wenceslas, somewhere in my mind I've met you and our lives intertwine. What favour is it that you want?'

SURREAL

His leather trousers creak as he relaxes by the fire. He sits in silence, feeding the flames until the first rays of sun fall on his sharp, bearded features. 'Come, sit. I have meat and bread in my pouch. We shall break our fast and I will tell you everything.'

He opens a brushed-leather wallet and offers it to me. 'Wait. I'll get ale.' He stands and goes to his horse, whispering to it, running strong hands along its flank.

He returns and thrusts a flask, black with pitch and shining from wax. 'Drink fast. I use this flask, my sister made it, but it leaks a little.'

From the wallet he draws coarse brown bread and dried venison. With ale and the warmth of a fire too — all is well with my strange world.

Wenceslas sits again, hands linked, elbows on knees. 'My land in this realm is fraught with tension, fire and instability; I dare not leave. I would that someone visit the rest and see that all is well.' He looks into the flames, yellow, orange and their shadows flickering across his prematurely care-worn features.

I wonder if there is more to this. 'What is your realm?' I ask.

He rubs his face, hands over his eyes — like he's hiding, not wanting to answer. Parting his fingers and looking into the flames, he says, 'You don't know?'

'No.'

He sighs. 'I am a Lord, but what does that mean? Surely we all have only one realm over which we hold dominion — our soul.'

'You want me to explore your *soul?*'

'Want you? I beseech you.'

'Why?'

He throws his hands in the air. 'Why? Because I am terrified, the soul is a big thing; there is brightness and dark in each of us. You could help me know myself. I lead people and could harm them through my ignorance.'

'That's the same for all of us. But if you let me into your soul, I may have terrible power over you.'

'And yet you may face great danger there and must be courageous. I prayed for an angel to take this task upon himself.'

'Or herself... But you got *me*. You poor man; I can't even walk from my office to the kitchen without screwing up.'

'I know not of what you speak, but you have been sent in answer to my prayers. Will you undertake this quest for me?'

'Not if you have a good lawyer… Fine then, yes; I'll look into your soul. Your generosity is legend, your kindness the subject of song. I'll try not to mess up. How do I enter your soul?'

'You do not know that you are already within it?'

'Ah, you mean your world is your soul.'

'How can it not be?'

I stand, grateful that the morning sun already offers a little warmth. Soft brown pine needles fall from my clothes and drift, glowing, through the fire. 'I am warm; the sun is up. I will leave now. Which way would you have me go?'

He stands too, walks round the fire and clasps my arm. 'Whithersoever.' Wenceslas releases me and strokes a calloused hand over the youthful hair of his beard. 'You may unravel the mystery of who you are and how you came here; I would know the truth of that, too.'

****

Walking east so the dawn falls on my face, I plan to head into the sun all day. It will lead me in a circle to the south. Maybe I'll return here as it sets.

Thin grey November clouds render the sun a pale disk that throws little shadow among the stark shapes of a stone circle on a low hill. Breezes make waves among the fine grass. There are no people here; it is bleak and stark. I push on into a frozen moor.

All is grey, black and white, a confusing pattern of grass, rocks, frost and snow. I'm surprised by the growl of a wolf ahead. Grey too; I could have walked right past without seeing it.

The wolf takes some paces forward — now I see it framed in snow.

Its head goes to one side, eyes stare up. 'You can see me?' it asks.

'Yes, wolf, I can.'

'All of me? My paws and rump too?'

'No, only your head and body, your tail and legs.'

'Then you are not in my world, but on the outside looking in. That is how it should be. Wenceslas would see all of me.'

'You have a message for him?'

SURREAL

'Only that all is well. Pass in peace, pilgrim.'

****

Don't ask me how I entered this next land — I don't know. I'm lying underwater looking up through the circled ripples made by dancing maiden flies.

Above the water, a ring of lintled stones circles this pond. The sky above is a perfect ultramarine, flowing to cobalt then to cerulean blue at the horizon. Exactly at the centre of the circle, a curl of cirrus hangs in a spiral.

Sitting up, I shed spangled droplets of glittering water and scatter the maiden flies. My clothes are saturated and heavy. My trainers squelch, but this place feels as if the season is high summer. The sun is much warmer here. I'm alone and strip off to wring my clothes out. No midges here, even by the water. I think I must be deep in the south, though I'm pretty sure I met Wenceslas far in the north.

The standing stones sit on a wide, grassy plain. I see no villages, smoke, roads or any evidence of the circle-builders. If this is part of Wenceslas then it is symbolic, ritual and quite beyond me to decipher. Well, nothing terrifying to report from here.

To the west, mountains soar. I abandon my plan, turn my back to the sun and jog towards the peaks.

The grass grows thicker here; daisies and dock give way to tormentil and bilberry. Ling and spicant sprout from cracks in exposed rock. Running for any time in jeans is not to be recommended and soon I'm wishing I was back in the cool water in the stone circle.

At last, *people*. Among the crags above, voices and echoes, people shouting. A burst of speed brings me to a man and boy each carrying a spear and dressed only in loincloths. Bare feet hiss through the grass and slap on stone. The two hunters dodge from side to side, trying to cut off the escape of an ibex. An ibex in Britain? I've heard of them in cave art — so I suppose they must have lived here. Maybe I've gone several thousand years back in time.

I slot into line with the man and boy so they don't have to work so hard. Other hunters have cornered the prey and we move forward. I get smiles and quick glances from the two hunters. I think they appreciate my help. Shouts from children and the clatter of thrown rocks drive the beast out of a cleft in the cliff above and the animal surges down scree towards us.

...you may face great danger and must be courageous...

Too right. I'm faint with fear, weak and trembling. This animal is huge, all muscle and terrifying ferocity. I join the two hunters in yelling and waving arms. The beast turns, confused. Spears, thrown by people hidden behind an outcrop of rock, pierce the ibex's white flank. It charges towards them and a young woman comes into view, scrambling with light, confident movements up a sheer crag and out of harm's way.

The man and boy run to a low cliff and climb. I follow. I presume the ibex is mortally wounded and there's no need for anyone to stay in danger.

'Courageous... right.' I stop shaking a little and follow them.

The two hunters settle on a shelf and chatter. Fast, tumbling words and laughter. I sit beside the boy. These two seem unsurprised to see me and I wonder why. I'm very different to them. I can't understand a word they say, but it doesn't stop them talking to me. More people appear above and clamber down to join us. My clothes, hair, everything is inspected minutely and the din of happy voices overwhelms me. These people smell sharp, peppery with an overlay of wood smoke.

A tall hunter, flanked by two others, stands about five metres from the stricken ibex, which struggles to rise. The hunter's left hand outstretched, the spear lying on it, his right hand cups the spear's end and aims the tip at the ibex's heart. The spear flies true and a few moments later the eyes of the prey glaze over. My crowded shelf is empty within seconds. About twenty people of all ages emerge from their safe places. Bags opened, they pull out stone knives and set about butchering their kill. I stand and turn away. I think I caught a whiff of the sea a moment ago. I'm off to look for it. I'll tell Wenceslas that all is well in these hills.

****

It's difficult to tell what time of day it is here by the sea. The light changes from moment to moment. The waves can be hissing phosphorescence in darkness one second and glittering in the sun the next. Not that I have a problem with this — it's beautiful. Nor am I complaining about the graceful and beautiful red-haired woman speaking to me as we walk side-by-side. The fact that she's wearing nothing is an added bonus as far as I'm concerned.

What surprises me most is that she leaves no footprints on the dunes, whereas I do. I suppose she's some sort of spirit, or symbol, rather than real. Her words seem to be made of random sounds, though they are full of meaning, conveying her mood, her reaction to me, or to our surroundings as they change.

We've been walking north for hours. In that time I've learned she's a relaxed, confident and warm person. Her hand is so gentle as she stops me, points to gulls squabbling for space on a rock, and laughs. She has a slow, lazy smile and tips her head a little to one side every time we look at each other.

Maybe she's magic and casting a spell on me and the world around. I've never felt so calm and content. She puts a hand on my shoulder, brushes away hair a gust has flicked across her eyes, and points north. A smile and soft words later, and she's walking away; back to the south. With her go the strange changes of light.

I'm standing in a blue dusk. Small waves hiss over rocks. About two hundred metres from the sea, up a gentle, rocky and heather-strewn rise, stands a curious house.

As I approach, I'm confused by one part that looks like a conservatory, but without roof or windows, merely a frame. Elegant and delicate, it looks as if someone meant it to be little more than decoration. Thick glass panels stand around a patio. A path, also lined with low slabs of glass, leads me to an arch through which I pass.

This part of the house is made of finely-hewn stone and the floor is rich and soft with blue coverings.

A girl races down a staircase and leaps for the central diamond pattern on a rug. It's quite a leap. For a moment, she's silhouetted against a tall stained-glass window. A white ribbon drops from her hand. Fluttering to the ground, its twists mimic the pattern in the window.

The hem of her knee-length dress bounces as she lands and skips in delight, clapping her hands.

She turns to me. 'I did it again! Hello, I'm Catherine and I'm eight years old. Who are you?'

I know Catherine; she's my daughter. 'Hello, Catherine, I'm a man sent by Wenceslas to look over his realm.'

'Wenceslas? Like in the carol?'

'The very man.'

She claps her hands again. 'Now I hear your voice, I know who you are.' She runs to me, grabs my hand and pulls me to the rug she landed on. Pointing through an arch she says, 'There you are.'

It's the strange, glassless conservatory she points into. A boy, about five years old, kneels on the carpet and plays with a boat.

Catherine says, 'I don't go in there very much. His imagination is too big and when he's playing boats my feet get wet.'

Indeed, the carpet is awash with tiny waves that carry the boat and hiss against shores around plant pots.

'I love this house. I come here lots to play,' says Catherine. She points to a headland across the sea. 'I went there once. It was very scary. When I looked back at the house it was so small, like I'd never be able to get in it again. But it grew back to its normal size as I got close. I think it must be magic.'

I look at the boy. 'That's me?'

'Don't you remember?'

'Sort of, but it was a long time ago. I made that boat, but must have been about ten or eleven. He looks a lot younger and I didn't play with it here.'

She laughs, 'Like you'd have noticed? He's away in fantasyland and only sees pirates and sea monsters.'

'I suppose you're right — and very astute. Tell me, have you any message for Wenceslas?'

'Tell him to come with his fiddlers three.'

'That was Old King Cole.'

'Oh yes.' She darts to her ribbon and snatches it up. 'I love the way the patterns keep turning up. All the same, but a little bit different.'

'You mean similar?'

'I must go and play. I won't be eight for ever. Bye!' She scampers up the stairs, the ribbon fluttering behind.

'Wait! Catherine,' I call after her. 'You will always be eight here.'

I turn and leave the house. Catherine has made things clearer. I think

I know where I am now — on the very edge of sanity. I wonder if Wenceslas sent me on this quest so that I would learn what *my* soul is and where the border lies between me and everything else — and why there's a border at all. So much is familiar here, and that gives me two problems. The first is that, if I'm right, I may not make it through the next land — I think I know what's coming. If I survive it, and those that follow, what the hell am I going to tell Wenceslas?

Night falls as I walk towards towering woodland. It's about to get bloody cold. Snatching up sheaves of dried grass, I stuff them into a thick layer between my jeans and my skin. My shirt gets the same treatment and my head a thick cap of moss.

Deep in a curve of the glen, I make a scarf of moss too, and wait for Winter.

I'm dying to see her, and that's the problem here: dying is all too easy.

She's tall, almost as tall as the trees, and strides with all the grace of the woman at the shore.

It's hard to see her. She has no body as such; only a form that distorts the world around her. As she moves, any part of her can seem to be made of rock, tree or air. In a moment she may stop and talk to me. But first… There it is; an orange flash, low, by the horizon. It disappears and returns with greater intensity, grows and sweeps through the sky in curtains of blues and greens.

Ice crystals grow from the edge of every leaf, creep up the bark of nearby trees as the woman nears them. The cold burns my face, squeezing tears from my eyes: ice on my eyelashes. It's hard to breathe.

'I won't stay long. I never do.' The woman's voice sounds far away and faint, as if having to crack its way through brittle air. Bark twists and falls in flakes as the cold distorts it.

She waves an arm to the horizon and up across the sky. 'You like my beautiful fire?' Shimmering curtains tease my eyes; how can something so vivid, so huge, be silent?

It's hard not to let my shivering turn to spasms of shaking. My teeth chatter and a thick mist forms every time I exhale. 'Winter…'

'Call me what you will. People fear me but gasp at my beauty. Some call me peace. I make total silence; no one else can do this. You need not attempt to imagine silence and stillness so perfect it destroys time and creates the eternal moment of beauty and truth, because it will be my gift to you. Some call me death and I kiss them from the filters of their cigarettes. Some think I'm far away, but I'm always close.'

I can hardly speak — my lips are like nerveless rubber. 'Please go. I have stopped shivering and that's a bad sign. I have never felt so cold.'

'Yes you have. I blackened your toes once. It took months for them to recover. Do you remember?'

'I do.'

'Farewell, pilgrim. You are not ready for my sweet kiss. Go to the shore; the fishwife has a fire to warm you. Tell Wenceslas that death is always a moment away.'

She strides deep into the wood and I struggle to move. It would be so easy to lie down here, to sleep just for a few minutes, but never to wake. Yes, I have met Winter before, but at least that time I was running. When I reached my house, only running muscles still worked. I could hardly stand and walking was impossible. I couldn't tell how hot the shower was when I crawled in and tried to warm myself up — the nerves in my skin had stopped working. I could have burned or frozen myself without knowing. So I wrapped myself in towels and lay on the floor, too weak and numb to take my frozen shoes off.

Keep moving! Oh God, this is so hard.

I think I can see a fire ahead, but it may just be the crimson alizarin of the northern lights where they touch the horizon. I can hear the sea.

Warm rain from the sea has fallen on frozen sand and formed a crust of ice that creaks and snaps under my feet. I've started shivering again — good, I'm on the road to recovery. There's the fire, the nets and the woman — another person sculpted from the elements around her. But with this figure the elements express mood. Where the sea around is calm, the waves in her are restless, the horizon stormy and clouded. I know why, she's worried: she always worries when her man is out to sea. Not frantic, not panicking, but, like all fishwives, she knows men sometimes don't come home.

'Hello, you,' she says as I kneel beside the fire. She wraps a blanket around me. I can't speak even to say thank you.

'You've come through Winter's fire? You must have seen Catherine. How is she? She owns me, doesn't she?' the woman asks. 'Look at you, you're blue.' The sea breeze flicks and snaps the shawl round her shoulders. She kneels beside me. 'Here, I have warmed soup for you. I knew you'd arrive with the dawn. And here you are, Mr Cold Man.' She rolls her eyes. 'I'm going to have to feed you like a baby. Ah well, all good practice for me. In my belly is a new life. Strange, when you give someone life you know they must die too. I condemn my child to death just as surely as my mother condemned me to it.'

She lifts an earthenware lid from a pot and stirs the contents with a spoon. Holding it to her mouth, she blows and the tip of her tongue flicks into the broth. A quick smile and glance at me, she says, 'Herring and barley. You'll soon be warm.'

My eyelids grow heavier with every mouthful. The shivering subsides and I curl up beside the fire.

****

I'm awake. The sky is darkening, the fire banked up to embers with fresh wood close to hand. The fishwife sits on rocks not far away. Wavelets wash over her feet. She's tossing things, bits of fish I think, into the air while gulls dart above her and catch them.

Rising, I fold her blanket and walk towards the rock.

'Hello, Mister,' she calls and points out to sea. 'There's his sail. Will he always come back?'

'Yes, but you will always worry. That's the way of things. Thank you for all you've done.'

She laughs. 'Tell Catherine to take care of me.'

'Oh, she treasures you. *I think*. But yes, she will care for you and love you more with every passing year — especially after I die.' I wave. 'Farewell.'

'Nice to have met you, Mister. You take care of yourself.'

I turn and walk towards a path. The sand gives way to concrete steps bordered by a low, stone wall. A ginger cat turns and blinks in the hot, bright sun — day, night and seasons follow unusual laws here.

'Hello, cat.' I stroke it. Hot fur and purrs. 'You died so long ago.' The cat doesn't seem to be aware of this and rubs its chin against my fingers.

I walk on. I'm looking forward to spring, to playing with the girls. Long dark hair and tanned skin from an outdoor life. They'll both smile a lot and pluck hawthorn leaves to feed each other, dance in front of cliffs covered in paintings of horses, deer and ponies. Something like that.

One of the girls will jump out at me…

'Tig!' she shouts, poking me. A flash of dark eyes and she darts away. I chase and try not to spend too long looking at her loincloth, that reveals so much of her bum.

I lunge. 'Tig!' and dodge her counter-attack. The other girl, maybe a twin of the first, joins in until I'm panting and exhausted. Sweat, so welcome after Winter and the northern lights.

'Where are you going?' the first girl asks.

'To see Wenceslas. Do you want to come too?'

'No, but we'll walk with you as far as the shelter.'

Life is good. The sun is warm, wood anemones grow between the exotic spikes of butterbur and I have a girl on either side of me. They each hold one of my hands and compete to push hawthorn and hazel leaves into my mouth. We leave the trees and enter a bare, rocky place. Beside it, branches support a turf shelter. Thin spirals of smoke rise from a damped fire.

'Look at our paintings!' The girls dance away from me and their shadows flit across the ochre and charcoal animals. 'Must you really go?'

'I must, but I will return and watch you. I do it so often.' I get a hug from both as I leave.

But my heart is heavy all too soon. I'm not sure if I'm going to cope very well with what comes next. I'm near the troubled realm of Wenceslas.

I grit my teeth and pass rough woodland, a castle on fire. A red pillar-box comes into view. A blond girl wearing a bright yellow T shirt ignores me.

A naked black girl stands in a desert of cracked and curled mud. She has her back to me and holds an AK47. I tell her there's no need for the gun. She looks at me, disbelief and contempt in her expression, and turns back to her fearful vigil. God knows what she's seen and done, but that look in her eyes tells me that I'm not man enough to help her cope with what can't be unseen and undone.

Fire, tank-tracks, a bomber drones overhead. I pass through a flattened and burned city. I shudder at footprints in the road. Someone ran across it even though the tar was melted at the time. There are no streets as such, just mounds of rubble.

Two German storm troopers haggle over a blanket. Both soldiers appear relaxed. Funny, when soldiers aren't fighting, they're just people.

Leaving them, I know I've come full circle. The air is cool again, chilling my skin. I hug myself and hope Wenceslas has a fire or a warm castle.

Neither. He's waiting for me in the wood and approaches on horseback again. The vapour of his breath drifts like phantoms.

'Well met. One year and a day,' he says. 'How long was it for you? You look older.'

'Merely tired... Exhausted actually. Your realm is as it should be, your lands too, including this one. There is conflict, doubt and despair here. This is where you are needed. There are warriors here; maybe you can stop the violence. One girl must break with her past and learn to cope. I don't believe I can help her. She needs someone who has had similar experience and come through it. I think she sees me as naïve.'

'I'll do what I can,' he says. 'You carry messages for me?'

'Only good wishes, though Winter warns us that death may be but a moment away. She is death, silence and stillness; you are life and change. No wonder there's conflict where you are; with change comes uncertainty, ignorance and fear. Winter may be in your soul, but you hold no power over her: you are opposite forces.'

'I am not human?'

'I've seen several humans here — all different. Hunters that see change; the passing of the seasons, hunger at times, food at others; danger and safety. But these are changes they expect. Winter is human too. The Fishwife and her husband know the stress of uncertainty: sudden death and despair. But you live in this land and choose to cope with the hardest changes of all — things you've never experienced and not prepared for. Wenceslas, you are ignorant, naïve and living in a world you do not understand: that makes you as human as it's possible to be.'

He dismounts and rests his forehead against the flank of his horse. 'You have taught me much.' Turning to me, he asks, 'Did you unravel the mystery of who you are?'

My heart freezes. This is the nub of the matter and I'm dizzy with the truth. It's like standing on the edge of a crumbling cliff. Winter's aurora surges through my mind. Cold fire, truth: deadly.

'Oh… yes…' I mutter, struggling not to speak of things I wish I didn't know. 'I learned too much and it is something that I cannot tell you. It would only make more mysteries and they are a waste of time. Winter's warning is enough. There's only one thing we can be sure of: *now*— this passing moment. That's all that exists. There is barely enough time to make the decision of how you are going to react to what is happening. Will we be brave, cowardly, generous, mean, loving or ignoring, or even cruel?'

'Winter is wise. I thank you for your help and your having quested for me.' He looks questioning, head tilted, lips pursed. 'You are restless. You wish to leave?'

'I must. Farewell, Wenceslas. You will not fail in your task here, though I cannot tell you how I know this.'

He clasps my arm as he did before. I turn and walk away, unsettled, back to my realm, my own little world. The truth tears me up inside.

To dream, imagine, to *create*… To have thought up and painted each of these pictures, hung them and walked through the exhibition. To have dreamed the thoughts and actions… given the people in each painting *life* and purpose, linked their lives within a story. Maybe I'll write it down.

My head roars, infinity and impossibility crashing together. I've walked to the edge of my soul and seen the madness, the chaos from which reality is made. Hopefully I can shut this vision down with the leaden cynicism and ignorance with which we ignore reality and stay sane — shrink our worlds until they're small, simple and safe.

Is creation the power of *gods?* If so, why is it in the hands of someone so confused and ignorant as me?

I thank my own creator for my thoughts, my feelings, my actions. The things that make me feel real and alive. I thank him or her for all their effort on my behalf.

And that Winter has still to come for me, and that, one day, she will.

BY THE THROAT

ALISON GARDINER

'AVENGE ME.'

Ashen face oddly expressionless, Duncan stared at Anthony. His hair was wild, as it had been in life. The bleeding gap where his throat had once been told the story of why Anthony could only see him in nightmares.

The sick feeling of horror that accompanied one of Duncan's visits clung to Anthony, stronger than ever, even as he struggled into wakefulness. Yet despite himself, he replayed his mental video of the last horrifying minutes.

'Avenge me.'

Over the past few weeks, Anthony had built a fragile acceptance of his brother's death. With those words, it splintered into shards.

Knowing there was no chance that he'd sleep again that night, Anthony rolled over and reached for his phone to see the time. It rang as he touched it. Maria's number flashed up.

'I'm frightened,' she said. 'I've had another awful nightmare.'

Anthony could envisage her sitting up in bed, phone clutched to her ear, spiky blonde hair in disarray, terrified blue eyes showing the fragility of her carapace.

Softly he replied, 'About Duncan?'

'Yes.'

'Me also. Tell me yours first.' He felt a heightened awareness as he invited her to open up. Each of her nightmares was usually identical, but possibly tonight her visitation had changed, as his had.

'The same. Staring down at me. But it's the throat. I can tolerate his eyes but not...' Her voice broke, tone ragged.

Anthony wasn't sure how she'd take what he had to say, but she needed to know. 'I understand. But listen. Tonight was different for me. He spoke.'

Maria gasped, her voice dropping to a whisper as if she were terrified of her own question. 'What did he say?'

'Avenge me.'

'What does that mean?'

Anthony clicked on the bedside lamp, filling his small room with a warm glow, yet failing to dispel his mental gloom. 'Perhaps Duncan's attempting to tell me that his death wasn't an accident.'

'Oh, Anthony,' replied Maria. 'I find the nightmares terrifying. I'm almost going out of my mind.'

'Me also.'

'But a dream is only a figment of the imagination. It's simply your feverish, unhappy mind trying to settle itself. Nothing more.'

Anthony wasn't surprised. He hadn't expected for a moment that she'd see it his way. 'Sorry, but I genuinely think Duncan is trying to get through to me.'

'Why would you believe that?'

'His words. If he were only a shadow in my mind, my mental processes re-shuffling, he would have said something different, like he was in pain or not at rest. He wouldn't have said, "Avenge me".'

The business-like note intensified. 'So you think that's proof he's trying to tell you he was killed?'

'Exactly. Until tonight I'd had no doubt that his death was a horrific accident. But this has got me wondering.'

'Two words are hardly enough to build a murder case on.'

He assumed her tone matched her expression; in Anthony's imagination, Maria began to look less frightened and more exasperated.

Anthony got out of bed and began pacing the floor, too restless to remain still. 'When I first had nightmares, his face looked all hazy, but latterly it's been getting more solid. It's almost as if he's been trying to gather strength to get through to this side. Maybe, finally, he's managed to summon the power to speak.'

'Why didn't you tell me that your nightmares had changed?'

Anthony tried to keep his voice calm and level, so wanting her to know he empathised with her, yet needing her to understand his point.

'I didn't want to frighten you. You might've expected your own to get worse.'

'This is getting really odd. You're suggesting that our dead brother has been on some ethereal plain gathering ectoplasm or something, so he can tell us to avenge his murder? I love you dearly but I need to be blunt about this. It's not very likely, Anthony. The whole thing would be laughable if it wasn't so macabre.' There was a slight pause. 'Anyway, the police seem to believe it was an accident. You've read what they've said in the papers.'

'Sometimes they're wrong.'

'So you're going to side with a ghost, a bizarre nightmare, against the highly refined scientific forces of the police? Take an aspirin and I'll see you in the morning.'

Anthony didn't have time to say 'I love you' before she was gone.

****

By daybreak, Anthony had put in three hours at his desk, sitting surrounded by newspaper cuttings, printouts and notebooks on which he had scribbled thoughts, questions, ideas. Exhausted, he picked up a photograph of Duncan laughing as he hugged a Great Dane puppy.

'Well, Duncan, who'd have thought that you'd die before Firedance? It doesn't seem fair.'

'Why do you call that dog Firedance, not Henry?'

His smile was already in place as he turned round. Maria was pale after her disrupted night, with dark shadows under her eyes, but he knew that his own face would be the mirror image of hers. The similarity between them facially was striking, even more so now that grief had been etched on both. Always close, they seemed to have been living out of each other's pockets during the last few appalling weeks.

'A bit of silliness really. When Firedance was a puppy, Duncan and I took him into the forest one day. The campfire had burned down to ashes when Firedance spotted something on the other side of the embers and charged straight across.'

'Ouch. Poor thing.'

Maria took the photograph out of his hand, smiling down at Duncan's happy face, curling her arm around Anthony's shoulders.

'He wasn't hurt, really. The fire had almost burnt out, but clearly there was enough heat to singe his paws. He was doing this hilarious high-stepping gait, like a cat on a hot tin roof, as he ran across the ash. It was like a bizarre modern ballet. So we called him Firedance.'

'I'm amazed you lived to tell the tale,' said Maria, putting the photo back on the desk. 'Sarah would normally have killed you for letting one of her puppies get into trouble.'

Anthony shrugged. 'She never knew. We kept using the name Firedance as a private joke between the two of us.'

'So the pair of you felt you needed something to bring out her fiery French temper? Not very wise. Coffee?'

'Thanks.' Anthony wiped his hands on his jeans, leaving a thin layer of glue on them. Carefully he picked up the newly stuck report and pinned it onto the noticeboard to one side of his PC, next to a map of the forest where Duncan had died.

Maria filled the kettle, then came over to look at the paperwork spread on his desk, idly picking up a newspaper photo. 'What are you doing?'

Removing the image from her hands, Anthony placed it exactly where it had been. 'Looking back over everything to see if anything might've been missed.'

'Wasting your time, dear. The police have been over every scrap of evidence. There's been nothing to show that it was anything other than an accident.'

'But they didn't know him like we did. There might have been something incongruous that they didn't recognise. Like if they had found a whip on his desk which they believed to be something to do with dog training, but we'd know it's not.'

Maria started drumming perfectly manicured nails on the desk, controlled patience in every tap. 'Okay, let's assume for a minute that I'm with you on this mad idea. We need to get access to the original police files.'

Anthony grinned at his sister. 'Now it's you who's talking crazy.'

'Maybe so, but I got it from you.' The kettle clicked off, as if to add emphasis to her final word.

'How do you expect I'll achieve this? Spot of cat burglary?'

Maria shook her head. 'My gym buddy, Helena, works at the

police station. She mentioned that the detective inspector in charge, Cuthbertson, was thinking of getting in a dog behaviour expert to try and get to the bottom of what happened.'

'That's one of the things I love about you. Even though you think that I'm not only barking up the wrong tree, but also wandering around in the wrong forest, you'll still kick your grey cells into action for me.' He hugged her hard.

'Of course. We've always stuck up for each other. In return, I expect your best coffee. I'll get the mugs.'

Anthony walked to the cupboard and started rummaging, trying to find some in-date filter coffee. 'But why would they want to get an animal handler in?'

'Everyone's terrified that the dog which killed Duncan might kill again —the papers are trying to squeeze as much drama as they can out of it. Cuthbertson wants a dog expert called in to help address the media frenzy.'

Triumphantly Anthony pulled out a packet of coffee and handed it to her.

Maria opened it, sniffed the contents, then began spooning coffee into the cafetière. 'Think about it. Now that Duncan's dead, *you're* the best dog behaviour authority locally. You could become the police expert on this case.'

Anthony gazed at her. 'Go on.'

'They'd let you look at all the files.' Maria was talking faster, face animated as she expanded her theme. 'You'd literally get access to everything. Photographs, times, places, all of it, even witnesses' testimonies.'

Somehow when Maria spoke, everything seemed easy, as if obstacles didn't exist.

'But do you think they'd take me on, seeing as I'm Duncan's brother?'

'Why not? Of course, Cuthbertson would need to know who you are. But relatives are required all the time to help police with their enquiries. And if you offer to work for a low rate, they'll snap you up.'

Anthony grinned as he held up his hand for a high five. 'Seems like a brilliant solution.'

'To something that's not even a problem? I've just dropped you into wads of work for probably no result. Yeah, I can see I've done you a real favour.' Maria handed him a mug. 'But if you're going to be so headstrong, I'll get Cuthbertson's number from Helena.'

****

'It's bizarre,' Cuthbertson said, deep, flat tones at variance with his words.

The heavy-set man opposite Anthony resembled a bloodhound with his sad dull eyes and heavily lined face.

'What?' asked Anthony. 'Inviting me here to help or the case itself?'

Cuthbertson shrugged his heavy shoulders. 'The whole thing. The fact that Duncan's throat was ripped out by a large animal, presumably a dog, yet no-one has reported their mutt going crazy or arriving home with a bloodstained muzzle, even after the news of the accident was made public.'

Anthony already knew many of the details, but he wanted to hear as much as possible directly from Cuthbertson. Hopefully he would let something slip or spark off an idea. 'So, what exactly is my brief in helping you on this case?' he asked.

'As a dog trainer you might be able to shed some light on whether this was a terrible accident or a carefully staged murder.'

Cuthbertson's voice was calm, but the word *murder* blasted adrenaline through Anthony, shooting his memory back to the day Cuthbertson had taken him to identify Duncan's body. Anthony had insisted on pulling the sheet back himself, unwittingly pulling it too far, giving him his first horrifying view of the gaping throat, creating the visual template that now shredded his nights. Deeply shocked, he had looked up at Cuthbertson's face. But even then the detective's eyes had been expressionless, face a mask. As now.

'Also, as Duncan was your brother I felt you might have a vested interest in helping me.'

'Oh yes,' Anthony murmured. 'I'd do anything to get justice for Duncan.'

The beetle-black eyes watched him closely as he asked the next question. 'What I need to know is whether a domesticated dog could be trained to attack so viciously.'

Anthony regarded Cuthbertson with interest. He knew from Helena that an excellent brain resided behind that bland middle-aged exterior. If Cuthbertson suspected that Duncan could have been murdered, clearly he had played his hand very close to his chest with the press, telling them little, making no suggestion of foul play. 'By somebody skilled, yes, given time and patience.'

Cuthbertson nodded. 'Could there be two people in this? Might one person have trained the dog, yet a third party have given the order to kill?'

'Absolutely. Once trained for a specific task the dog would take orders to perform it from anyone else. Over the training period there would need to be some sort of practice runs. Have there been any other dog attacks reported over the six months before Duncan died? Not necessarily to humans, maybe to other animals.'

'That's an interesting question. There have been quite a few, although nobody actually hurt or killed. Except in one case, about two weeks before Duncan died. Let me get the file.'

Cuthbertson tapped a few commands into his computer. As he did so, Anthony had a proper look round the office. It was old fashioned, with dark wood furniture, navy velvet curtains. Cuthbertson must have fought progress hard to stand still in time so efficiently. The only concession to the impact of the last fifty years seemed to be the mobile phone on his oak desk and the computer. Cuthbertson grunted approval at the screen, then swung it around towards Anthony.

Anthony began to read Constable Barnes' file report aloud. 'A woman out walking her poodle near the lake in Arneworth Forest…'

'Same location,' muttered Cuthbertson.

'…was terrified when an enormous black dog bounded out of the trees and attacked her poodle, ripping its throat out. Mrs Tennant claimed that the dog's owner had acted in a totally irresponsible fashion. The poodle had been hit by a tennis ball, which she presumed had been thrown by the black dog's owner. Terrified, she had screamed at the man, as his dog was charging after the ball, aiming straight towards them. The owner was calling the dog's name, George, even before it attacked, but the dog paid no attention. Mrs Tennant wants the killer dog destroyed as she feels it was dangerous and out of control. She intends to put in a formal complaint against its master for murder of her dog and bolting, not stopping to offer any help.'

'You needn't bother reading the rest,' said Cuthbertson, swinging the screen back. 'It goes into considerable length about the woman's distress at being left alone in the forest with the corpse of her dog.'

Anthony leaned back in his seat, frowning. 'It certainly sounds as if the lady owner had a point about both the dog and its master. Was she sure it was a man?'

'No, she couldn't be positive. The figure was wearing a coat and a hat. She made the assumption owing to the person's height and the masculine clothing.'

'What's happened so far? Did you find the culprit?'

Cuthbertson frowned, the first emotion he had shown. 'Not yet. Normally something like this wouldn't take up a huge amount of police time but, owing to the potentially dangerous nature of the dog and the callousness of the owner, we took it very seriously. We checked with Duncan's kennels first, being the biggest around. His wife assured us that there were no black dogs on site, neither was there one called George. We checked with all the other local kennels. We involved the local media — TV news and press — but we drew a blank. Finding that dog and owner is vital.'

'I'll give it some thought,' said Anthony, getting up stiffly. 'I'll start by going back over to Duncan's kennels and talking to Sarah about the dogs in this neighbourhood. Whether my non-grieving sister-in-law will be helpful or not remains to be seen. I assume she's a suspect?'

'Number one. No proof. Currently it's still a terrible accident. Unless you can shed some light otherwise.'

****

Hanging over the kennels' entrance gate, Anthony watched as Sarah hosed down a muddy Great Dane. She'd glanced up as he'd arrived, then immediately returned to the task in hand.

'Hello, Firedance,' called Anthony.

The dog looked up and wagged its tail.

Sarah's hard eyes showed no sign of welcome. 'Why don't you just lose that stupid name?'

'All right. Hello, Henforth Bandolier Montgomery the fourth.'

'Not his kennel name. Call him Henry, like normal people. What do you want?'

Anthony ignored the belligerent tone. 'Information. The truth.'

'That fool of a detective sent you over here didn't he? Too lazy and stupid to do his own work is he? I've no intention of talking to you. Get off my premises. This is my place now.'

She straightened up, her tall angular frame making her look like an aggressive stick insect. Wrenching Firedance hard by the collar, she dragged him around to wash down his other side, ignoring the yelp as she stood on the dog's paw.

Anthony's eyes narrowed. 'Firedance is an animal with feelings. Can't you treat him any better than that?'

'It's how I treat all animals. Including humans.' She sprayed the dog's flank with the hard jet of water, gripping on to his collar as the animal twisted to get away.

'Total lack of compassion is not a great attribute.'

Reaching for the tap she turned up the jet of water, looking Anthony straight in the eyes. 'Is there something you want to say? I have no time to stand here and listen to your petty opinions.'

Anger pounded through Anthony but he kept his face expressionless, tone flat. He wasn't going to give her the satisfaction of knowing that she'd got to him. 'It'll only take a couple of minutes. I've come to find out if you know anything about the poodle attacked by a dog some weeks before Duncan's death.'

She went on relentlessly hosing Firedance down, even though he already looked clean. 'Nothing. Why would I?'

'Because you know many of the dog owners around here, either through the kennels or your training programs. I thought maybe you'd have heard something.'

'Same questions as that detective. Strangely enough, asking twice won't get you a different answer.' Sarah switched off the water and stood back as Firedance shook himself. 'I still don't know anything at all about the black dog or the poodle. Get lost before I get Henry to chase you off my land.'

The Great Dane's ears pricked up as he heard his name.

'That's generous-spirited, Sarah. Setting a dog on your own brother-in-law.'

Sarah spat on the ground. 'Well, ex-brother-in-law really, as the only connection between us is now dead. Fini. But what I'm actually getting the dog to do is run off an intruder, a nuisance, harassment. In fact, I believe the police are supposed to protect me against that sort of stuff. Ironic, really, if you now work for them.' She dropped onto her knees by the enormous dog's head, holding his collar, voice becoming soft but menacing. 'And if you are not clear of these premises in two minutes, I will release Henry.'

'It's amazing that Duncan married you. You've nothing in common with any of us.'

'Tennis, dogs and love of French food. Thankfully nothing else. One minute.'

Disgusted, Anthony turned and walked away. It was tough to now be a totally unwelcome visitor in his childhood home. Seeing it again intensified the hollow feeling he'd been carrying since Duncan's death, as if something were missing, something precious had been lost. If it hadn't been for the final spectacular argument with his father, when he and Maria had flatly refused to take over the dog training business, the old man would never have bequeathed the property outright to Duncan. Secretly the three siblings had agreed to share the property rights once their father had died. When Duncan married Sarah, she had become his heir. Duncan had loathed Sarah after her affair, finally seeing past her smoky French accent and animal passion, but he had never got around to writing a will excluding her.

With Duncan's death, Anthony and Maria had lost more than just their brother and soulmate; they'd lost all chance of regaining their family home.

****

He phoned Maria as soon as he got home, giving way to his desire to rant about Sarah.

Maria remained calm. 'So, we need to find that dog without her. But I'm not sure how. If there's already been a public campaign and the big kennels know nothing about it, the dog probably isn't from around here. It might have been brought in from another county.'

'That might explain why there have been no other local attacks. Their trial runs would have taken place elsewhere. I'll ask Cuthbertson to search the police files in neighbouring counties and see if anything crops up.'

Two hours later he phoned Maria back. 'He's checked nationally. There's nothing. We're back to square one.'

Preparing for bed that night, Anthony found that he didn't have his usual feeling of dread about Duncan appearing. If Duncan had been murdered, another visit from him might help.

Yet when the dawn softly spread its blanket of light across his duvet, Anthony woke from a deep and refreshing sleep undisturbed by any visions.

'I need your help, Duncan,' he murmured to the misty early morning horizon. 'I believe you were killed; only I don't know how.'

Maria had passed an equally undisturbed night; she rang early. 'If Duncan won't come to you in the night, you've somehow got to get to him by day.'

'Hold a séance or something?'

'No, nothing as crude as that. Immerse yourself in everything he had. His old trunk, his diary. Go to the places where he went. Sit among his stuff and think.'

'That's easy for you to say. You're not trying to make contact with a murdered spirit.'

'It's not me who believes he was bumped off. I'm willing to help, but I'm absolutely not going to try and call up his ghost.'

'OK. If you need me, you'll probably find me sitting on his grave or something. Wish me luck.'

Feeling in equal parts unsettled and stupid, Anthony went up to the attic to dig through the boxes of Duncan's personal stuff which he'd collected from Sarah, knowing she'd just bin them. It was an eclectic mix of stuff: photographs of the three of them playing together as children, postcards, feathers, newspaper cuttings, yellowed theatre programs, the order of service from their father's funeral. Leafing through, he tried to keep his mind open, hoping that some idea would pop into his head. Perhaps he'd find a note that Duncan had written before he died. Anything to give him a clue. A new will would help. Yet despite three hours of sifting through Duncan's possessions, including a trunk of old clothes, he was unable to find anything of note.

Exasperated, he gave up and went downstairs for lunch. The weather was closing in rapidly. He'd left a beautiful sunny morning as he had gone upstairs but now heavy, dark clouds hung overhead. As Anthony opened the back door, a shard of lightning shafted the sky, an angry score across the heavens. Out of habit, Anthony started counting to see how long it would be before thunder arrived. Five seconds.

His mind went back to a time long ago in Jamaica, when he'd stood with Maria and Duncan, riveted by a storm much angrier than this one. All of them had been terrified, hanging onto their father as he crouched beside them, explaining about the weather. 'Knowledge cures fear,' his father had said.

It hadn't cured it for them that night. After they'd been put to bed, Maria had crept through from her own room and Duncan had slid down from the upper bunk. Together they'd huddled in Anthony's bed, listening to the storm outside, frightened, but comforted by being together.

As Anthony started to pull the back door closed, a sudden gust of wind ripped it out of his hand, slamming it against the wall beyond. The wind shot through the kitchen, ruffled open the pages of a magazine on the table, then died.

The hairs on the back of Anthony's neck stood up as fear wrapped its icy fingers around his heart. This was weird. Why had the wind suddenly blown up like that? How could it disappear so suddenly?

Shaken, he shut the door and locked it. He stood for a moment staring at the magazine. Was this Duncan's message? Bathed in cold sweat, hands shaking, Anthony reached towards it.

The magazine had fallen open at an article about planting petunias. Puzzled, Anthony read it twice but nothing stood out. His heart rate began to fall as his adrenaline levels subsided. He looked back out at the storm-ridden night.

'What is it, Duncan? What are you trying to get me to see?'

He glanced back down at the magazine and suddenly it struck him. A small advert in the bottom right-hand corner of the page. It featured Dr Owen's black hair dye. Anthony started to laugh.

****

Sarah strode out of the kitchen with Firedance as Anthony's car crunched down the gravel drive. She stood with her feet planted, dirty brown oilskin coat flapping around her knees, glaring at him. This time Anthony made no attempt to open the gate, choosing not to invite her aggression.

'Back again?' she shot at him before he'd had a chance to say a word. 'The answers to the questions haven't changed. Goodbye.'

For once her rudeness didn't affect him. 'Actually it's the questions that have changed. I came over here last night. I thought I'd have a bit of a look round.'

'That's trespass. Illegal.' The tone was as harsh and unforgiving as usual but a degree of wariness had crept into her face. 'I'm alone, but I'm not without protection.' She jerked her head towards Firedance, who stood wagging his tail.

Anthony ran an eye over the sprawling farmhouse beyond Sarah. 'Let's put it down to sentiment, as this was once my home. You might be interested to see what I found in the barn.'

He held up a plastic forensic bag containing the remnants of a packet of black hair dye.

'And what of it?' asked Sarah, pulling Firedance close to her side.

'The old cubbyhole in the rafters seems a strange place to find it. If it was yours, you'd have kept it in your bathroom. Duncan and I always put our secret things in that cubbyhole as kids. Presumably he showed you our hiding place.'

'Maybe. And so?'

Anthony could feel that his point had struck home. She was listening intently now, needing to know how much he knew. 'It's the kind of dye that washes out immediately. So if a dog dyed black with this swam in a lake, perhaps in pursuit of a stick, maybe even ducking its head under to look for a stone which had been thrown, it would come back out its normal colour.'

The face remained closed, her tone sarcastic. 'Well done, Sherlock. Any other startling revelations?'

Anthony pocketed the bag and indicated the Great Dane. 'Firedance is huge. He could be trained to rip out a man's throat. But he would have to have a clear indication of the intended target. Pointing would be too inaccurate. He might see a squirrel beyond. You'd need to hit the target with something you could throw accurately.' Anthony reached into his pocket and produced a tennis ball. 'Like this.'

Sarah kept her hand firmly on Firedance's collar. Her eyes were threatening as she said, 'Carry on with this fairy story.' She looked more alert and focussed than Anthony had ever seen her, body rigid, eyes fixed on his face.

'Also you'd need a verbal cue. Something that wouldn't come up in everyday life, as you couldn't risk the dog hearing the word and attacking at the wrong moment. You're French. It suddenly clicked that what the poodle woman had heard was not George, but *la gorge*. The throat.'

Sarah laughed, a harsh guttural sound. 'Total conjecture. No possible proof. I've listened long enough to your ridiculous story. Clear off or the dog attacks.'

There was no doubt in Anthony's mind that it would. Sarah's dogs were all trained to obey orders without hesitation. Yet Anthony felt no fear.

'If Firedance does attack, he'll be put down and you'll be fined heavily, probably will never work with dogs again. If he actually kills me, even the slow-witted police will work out what happened. Guilty of two murders.'

Sarah gave a short impatient shake of her head. 'Nobody could prove that I'd done it intentionally. I'll inform them you were threatening me. Using the dog would be self-defence in law.'

'Not for you, it wouldn't be. Not if it proves the guilt of the first offence.'

'Let that false thought be a comfort for you in your final few seconds of life. But remember, no proof means no conviction. That goes for any crime. Even murder.'

Her fear was beginning to show, pupils wide, forehead sweaty. She must suffer more. Anthony pushed on. 'The dog's training will be its own evidence. I've only got to show Cuthbertson what he can do. It should be clear to the jury how you carried out Duncan's murder.'

'Pity dogs don't live long, isn't it?' Sarah pulled a small canister out of her coat pocket. The trademark colours of Hardacre's Rat Poison were clearly visible. In a swift movement, Sarah levered off the lid and started pouring the contents into a dog-food bowl.

Anthony reached for the gate, trying to wrench it open. The heavy catch was stiff against his fingers and he still had the yard to cross. Firedance was already approaching the bowl, salivating. Anthony would never make it.

'You malicious witch,' he yelled. 'That dog served you faithfully, yet you reward him with death.'

Her face was hard, with a strange wild look in the eyes. 'More conjecture.' She didn't even have time to drop the canister as the tennis ball hit her.

'La gorge!'

Firedance –
The Ragged Dancers

T F Grant

THREE RAGGED CHILDREN GYRATE TO RHYTHMS that none can hear. Out here on the edge, looking down into the abyss, dancing, hopping, spinning between the cracks in time. A place without form except for the bloody velvet darkness beneath their feet. A suffering silence surrounds them as they dance on the fractured fractals of reality. Hopping from stuttering thread to fluttering spreading unctuous light, falling away into the silence; a silence relieved by the music of their feet.

A swollen light. A blister forms to the beat of their feet, their repetitious feet. Their hanging breath a mist in the flow from past to future, through their present, always their present; everything is present to them for they are the ragged dancers and they dance to the beat, the slow solemn beat, of the universe.

The abyss quivers into the blister flowing upwards, breaking, a cresting wave of warm life-force, unfortunate, inopportune, incessantly squirming into the scalar chaos of existence. As below so above, as above so beside, as beside so within; the universe trembles to the sigh of a dancing breath upon its soul.

To travel, but never to leave this spun dark moment in the beginning and end of it all, at the point where all flashed into existence and all faded into heat-death. To be but not to believe in anything at all, no words within, no sound without, just the rhythm, the beat, the glissading notes glistening into the fullness of it all. To wonder, to wander, to be all things to all people, to make the fire, the animating fire, that which gives life to that which gives everything back in return.

So they dance on the cracks of the universe above the aching void of the abyss.

And call it fire dancing.

****

You awake, cold and grey, in a light lashed cloud. An illuminated mist that flows away from you, to you, around you, within you, everything at once, all your lives focused on this spot, this choking symphony of time. You gasp, a shuddering breath in and out, the tidal spasm breaching, breaking, curling within you, boring you out and leaving only echoes in its wake. You weep, tears seeping, sliding, pouring from your eyes, those windows closed to the void to avoid the pain churning throughout the abyss.

You speak. 'Where am I?'

They answer, a solemn wind pouring through your soul. 'Nowhere.'

'It's dark here.'

'Let the light shine through you.'

'I don't understand.'

'Open your eyes and look.'

'I died.'

'Many times. Open your eyes and look.'

'I'm scared.'

'No matter. Open your eyes and look.'

You open your eyes and look.

Three ragged children dance about you, slow circles, widdershins and spinwise, toward the light and away, granting you sight that sees…

…you have died as a child, as a baby, as a man, as a woman, cold and lonely, warm and loved, in battle, and in rest. You have created evil in the world. You have granted joy to the world. You have been a singer, a dancer, a killer, a poet, a lover, a beast, a fool, a wise man pontificating on what he could not comprehend. The lives swallow you up and you drink them down, your throat open, your soul filling. Threads of gold, of night, of sun, of days spent churning through your life, illuminated, obscured, enlightened, repressed, all that you have been, would be, could be, and are.

A broken thought made whole and filled up with the fire of the deep, the deep time, the deep space, the place, nowhere and everywhere.

They sing the notes and dance the steps and you scream for mercy, but they do not play such games, not them, not the ragged dancers.

You have lived as an insect, a fish, a lizard — a huge roaring lizard thundering terror onto the world — as a rodent, a bird, a horse, an elephant. All things, you have lived as all things for all time, evolving, changing, clawing your way up the tree, and at each branch your soul grew. You have known misery and hope, warmth and cold, hatred and love. All things come, all things go, and you remember them all.

'What am I?' you screech.

'Life.'

'Where am I?'

'No where.'

'When is this?'

'No time.'

'Tell me what you want.'

'We want nothing, seek nothing, see nothing, we simply danced and you came as a blister on the void.'

'But there must be a reason.'

'A reason. Ah yes. A reason. Life is one moment in time, leading to another, to other places, other whens like this. We do not live. We do not die. We do not understand what these things mean. We conjure you to answer the question.'

'What question?'

'Why?'

'Why what?'

'Why do we exist? Why do you exist? Why does the abyss exist? Why does the fire, the indivisible fire, exist?'

'I don't understand.'

'Then you shall have to return and discover the pain anew. Comprehension is pain, and requires your compliance.'

You fall then, the abyss swallows you whole, and the ragged dancers dance.

****

A cold black hardtop shimmers away, glistening wet with dust-spun tears. You see the world in shades of rosé until time breaks hard against you. All the blues is: is a good man in hard times. And times are hard, broken hard, spoken hard, choking hard, screaming into your soft featherbed soul, as all crumbles into a glistening tear-strewn highway through the dust of your past.

The past submerges all that you are, were, could ever be, but you never had the eyes to see. Value meaningless a zero sum in your gaze so fixed upon the price. Not for you to care about the ragged children lost upon the streets of hometowns destroyed by the micro-second trades that tore out the soul of the nation and made all weak, all lost, until the day it came to your door and then, and then, and then, you saw.

Cast out, surplus, ivy-league worthless, in a world playing gamification in a crowd-sourced, crowd-funded, crowd-weighted tyranny of the banal. A master of the universe crashing through the wrong percentage point and out onto the streets where tents are banned by imperial edict.

Hunger.

Thirst.

And knowing you are worth less than a man who didn't go to school but knows how to fix things up real cool. You can quote Gecko, but he can build a house, fix a machine, drive a nail, cure a ham, knows what to do when his gun jams. He fought in your wars while you snorted and cavorted and made your deals for the oil, the spoils, the cost not a problem in a cost-plus excavation of the pride of the nation.

You scrabble in the dust, a bean-counter out-counted by a silicon fiend. You grope for a purpose, a soul-less, suit-less, shill without a friend to call, to help, they all stall, and look away, because you're not one of them anymore, your value is only judged by your price. You scratch along a broken tarmac track and find God, ah God, yes your saviour, shout out your sins, and they take you in, but you still have no soul, just a hole where once you coveted.

These goodly people, godly people, people of long hair and long songs chanted in the treeless forests that you created, take you in, accept your sin, make you a home, put you on your feet, and you see it, right there, right there in front of you, a place, a way, to make your mark. Revelation, divination, exultation to a higher power you never felt in the soul you never believed existed.

There are always sheep.

Wolf-cold eyes you have now, a white powdered nose, a stack of good books, and a lush deal in the marketplace of hell-fire and damnation.

Ah but you misjudge when you send out your tough men, your righteous men, your signed-up and paid-for men, to take out the right-seeing eye that offends you.

Take a goodly man, a godly man, a man who knows right from wrong, short from long. His tale in the telling but shattered by the felling of the tree that existed from the start of it all. Now away he falls as they come to his door and tear his eyes right from his head in the hope that he won't see so clearly anymore. But his clear voice is strong, raised up in song, telling the tale to the poor, the dispossessed, the powerless, but people are power, and now the flames rise, rise, rise at your door.

Scrabble, scrabble, little doggie, you made this pit now watch it close and crumble in upon you. The dark mass of your life-choices suffocating all that you could have been, should have been, would have been, if you had chosen the honest path.

And above, quiet as distant thunder, children dance.

****

It is someday — for time loses meaning, its flow stopped by hunger and despair, starvation eats when you do not — and you stand silent, numbed by grief upon a naked hillside in the heated air. Your children, fruit of your womb, lie tumbled at your feet, alive but barely, withered by famine, no tears left to flow. You stand and look across the parched earth and wonder where to go.

Your man is gone, dust on the wind; he fought until the last, but all he did was lost to this world when the rains did not come to pass. With naked gaze you waited for a sign from anywhere and yet... nothing came, no God to call, so you made your gruesome bet.

With your stumbling children, and one held in your arms, you stagger in a direction born of fate. Each night you spin a strange-shaped stone, like a needle fine and fair; where it stops that way you go, and hope to find a share.

On you walk. You drink from ditches, puddles, no ponds to find. With aching hunger and bloody stools you follow the stone's design. Onward, onward, 'cross the earth, spin, spin, take a step and then another. In this dance, you must find one small place to give your dwindling fruit a chance. Not for yourself, you do not care if you live or die, but just a chance for all that's left; a child with his father's eyes.

One more step and then another and finally you top the rise, that last rise, and ah before you lies... a city of tents. A cry of hope in a fractured world. Sanctuary.

Your child's stick limbs can no longer carry the weight of his bloated body, so you lift him once again and stagger onward to the lines.

That child, your only child, all that's left from that withered vine. The child with his father's eyes. The child you carried with your last breath. That only child survives.

And laughs, and plays, and learns the way, to be a man, like his father was, and help, and live, and build again.

And below, as water babbles in a brook, children dance.

****

You gurgle happiness into your father's heart and bask in the warmth of your mother's love. First steps, first words, first tantrum. Your mother firm, strong, holds you to account for your actions. Your father stern, tough, makes you clean up your mess despite your wailing cacophony of me, me, me.

Us, us, us, is the law of love, the law that makes all things possible. Me will break the world, us will mend it; I will make the choice and we will suffer the result good or ill, so choose wisely, choose with your heart, your mind, your soul.

You grow older, the beat of life unstoppable while the blood still flows. You learn that words are made of letters. You learn sums are made of numbers. You learn that some sums are made of both; the language of the universe opens its heart to you.

This word goes here. This verse goes there. Is this a real song, a song of infinity, tearing open all upon this prescient sea? Raggedly you search for the solution, for the proof; all you need is proof, proof of love, proof of truth, proof that the universe makes sense.

A step, another step, and all opens before you.

Now comes the choice: keep the secret, dole it out, make your fortune on the back of other men; or give it away, allow all to use what you have discovered — this thing that will change the world.

Make your choice.

And beside you, like woven lines, children dance.

****

God does not exist. God does exist. The universe exists but does god exist? God with a capital or a lower case, god with a capital city or no place, god with genitalia or immune to hormonal chance. God, god, goddess, godly, godling, go find a world of your freaking own.

Infinity exists, infinity is real, the number line extends and we follow where it points. It's not an open question, it's not a question at all, not with real numbers breaking the world into an infinity of tiny, tiny, tinier pieces. Fractions make fractals, fractals make patterns, patterns the same no matter where you stand in the picture frame.

Don't look at where it is, look at where it is going. Don't look at where it is going, look at where it is. Uncertain of your place in the world, well now think, think, think on this.

Infinity means anything that can happen will. Implausibility is part of infinity's game. Plausible is finite, concrete, solid, a probability plotted; infinity is without end, without beginning. It extends but it does not comprehend. We have small brains, small minds, but let us see what, by thinking, we can find.

Anything that can happen will: god exists, god doesn't exist, a feature of the number line. To exist and not exist at the same time is to exist in a superpositional space within infinity's mind.

Think on.

A superpositional god would not have a fixed point in space or time, would not have a truth that is true for every mother-loving kind. A superpositional god would encompass everything and nothing: choose Pagan, Mithran, Christian, Jewish, Muslim, Buddhist, Hindu; choose deist, theist, agnostic, atheist; choose seeking or choose being as closed-minded as a holy book flung upon a fire.

Nothing matters. God, the superpositional being that exists and does not exist in all of time and space, has a place for you in the quantum infinity's worldview.

A blown mind is an open mind.

Think on.

Think on heaven. Think on hell. Many ways to find the mansion and sup from the endless well. But how can all be right and all be wrong?

How can you go to the heaven of your faith and the hell of another's? How can your soul disintegrate in agnostic disbelief and, at the same time, return in reincarnated relief? Transmigration, conflagration, dissipation, heavenly reciprocation, all at the same time, in one ragged soul, torn in so many places at once, burning, birthing, singing with a harp upon a cloud so bright.

The answer so sure, so obvious, so pure: if your soul is split in many directions then it too is superpositional and immune to your reflection. Your mortality, your life, is a cage for the soul, the collapsed quantum soul, held tight within your mortal shell, then released with your final breath to fill all the niches of creation.

Do you see it yet? Does it glimmer for you?

If god is superpositional and the soul is superpositional and the universe exists without time inside space? For that is what infinity means. Time is not a concept that infinity can stand, space has no reality in infinity, there is no place, no when, no how. Do you see? There is just infinity — infinitely divisible infinity.

God, soul, no time, no place, and the ragged three dancing on the fractal line. Black box testing the universe. How many paths, how many ways to live, to die, to travel, to stay, to love, to laugh, to cast it all away, to kill, to heal, to pleasure, to feel? All lines, all ways, all infinite in their variety and all there. Lines on the soul of the universe.

There is no god, there is no soul, there is only…

You.

And three ragged children gyrate within it all.

MESSING WITH FIRE

ALF HAYWOOD

LUKE MCGREGOR WAS VISITING HIS PARENTS in Chicago for a few days, a short break before he was due to be sent overseas again. His family and a few close friends knew he was in the army, but no one else; they probably wouldn't have cared anyway. His family still thought of him as the quiet, shy boy he used to be because he never told them anything about his career or what he did. After completing his basic training he transferred to a specialist unit; he told his family it was just a routine desk job.

When his father started shouting at the reporter on the television one evening, he tried to explain what the liaison officers were attempting to do in that Arab country.

'Yeah right, you do all your fighting from behind a desk. What the hell do you know about that place?' his father had bellowed. If it hadn't been for that little argument he might never have gone for a walk to calm down; or met his future wife.

It was about an hour later, and getting dark a little early because of the heavy rain clouds blowing in from the southwest. He walked slowly and steadily, wondering, yet again, whether he could trust his parents with the truth about his real job. A quick glance along the road revealed a young girl on the same sidewalk. She looked about twelve or thirteen years old and with each step closer, she bounced a tennis ball into the air and then caught it again. They were about thirty yards apart when she missed a catch and sent the ball careering high into the air and across the road.

The girl stayed where she was, rather than chase the ball, and nothing more should have happened. Unfortunately, the ball bounced off the hood of a passing limo that screeched to halt. The driver and his passenger both jumped from the car and while the passenger examined the spot where the ball struck, for damage, the driver retrieved the errant ball.

'This ball yours kid?' the heavyset passenger called, clicking his fingers for the driver to hand it to him.

Frightened of what the man was going to do or say the girl simply nodded her head, before adding quietly, 'I'm sorry, it was an accident.'

'Sure kid,' he replied without a trace of emotion. 'Come get your ball.'

Just as she stretched out her hand to take the ball, he seemed to reconsider his decision to hand it back. She watched him lift it high above her in one hand and then as he brought it down again about a foot from her face, he sliced the ball in two with a knife that appeared from nowhere in his other hand. She looked a lot more frightened as she stared at the two halves of the ball dropping from his open palm onto the asphalt road. She froze completely when he grabbed one shoulder and began to flourish the blade close to her face; she stood petrified like a rabbit dazzled in a bright light.

With a voice full of hatred and malice he threatened her: 'Ya gotta learn a lesson kid, you mess with me, and you're messing with fire.'

The lighthearted words that came from his side took him by surprise: 'She's kinda small for a guy like you. Why not pick on someone a bit bigger?'

They forgot the kid in an instant as both men tried to assess the intruder. With a dismissive shrug of his shoulders, Mike Cossanti ordered his driver to deal with him. 'Hurt him, Gus, teach that freaking do-gooder to mind his own business in future.'

Gus stood at least six foot two or three and was built like a tank. In three enormous strides, he reached Luke and drew back his fist to start reshaping his face, but then it all went wrong. Luke wasn't there when he threw the punch; instead he felt an agonizing blow to his crotch from where Luke was kneeling below him. Gus doubled up instantly, gasping for breath and defenceless. Luke sent him crashing to the ground seconds later with a harsh chop to the back of his neck that ended the 'fight' in about three seconds.

Cossanti's eyes registered his shock at what happened in those seconds, then he reached inside his jacket for a more powerful weapon, calling out, 'You son-of-a-bitch, I'll teach you to mess with Mike Cossanti. I'm gonna…'

He was still yelling obscenities when Luke's well-placed drop-kick sent him and the revolver sprawling onto the road. He had barely made it to his knees when a second kick to his kidneys sent him back to the floor to writhe in agony.

He stopped rolling when the sole of Luke's shoe pressed on his tonsils; he peed his trousers when Luke knelt closer and held the knife across his mouth to stop him begging for mercy. He only started screaming when Luke cut a small piece from the end of Mike's nose. 'You're lucky I'm in a good mood, Cossanti. Next time I'll cut off something a lot more painful — if I can find it.'

Luke left Cossanti blubbering on the floor and nursing the disfigured face in his blood-soaked hands. He walked over to collect the revolver and send the girl away, but she was already long gone.

Luke smiled and nodded his head in approval. 'Smart kid that, I hope I'd have done the same at her age,' he said to no one in particular before walking away.

****

For the next seven months, Cossanti repeated his threat over and over: 'I don't care how long it takes or what it costs. I want him found so I can cut his innards out. Yeah, and I'm gonna cut that punk's heart out last of all, when he's begging to die.' Then he sent out more of his henchmen to find Luke.

When Luke eventually returned home, he had long since dismissed the incident as a minor affair that no longer concerned him. He might have been a lot more careful if he'd known how many people were trying to find him. Crude artists' impressions sat under the counters of almost every shop — along with the offer of a big reward in and around the neighborhood.

A simple co-incidence finally ended the search.

Luke was out walking and dropped into a small convenience store for a paper, when he bumped into the girl. She was engrossed in her new magazine instead of watching where she was going.

'Weren't you bouncing a ball the last time we met?' Luke asked after he recognized her.

The girl looked a little frightened for a moment but then relaxed. 'Yes, I'm sorry I ran away but those men scared the hell out of me. Once you were OK I ran for my life.'

'That's OK. It was the right thing to do. They weren't so tough anyway. Another year or two and you wouldn't have needed my help to flatten them.' He looked up to see who might be listening to the conversation. The young cashier switched his stare away from Luke and tried to hide one hand behind his back while looking as innocent as he could.

'Stay there for a moment,' Luke ordered the girl, before advancing towards the startled youth. After a very brief argument Luke examined the crude drawing. It wasn't a brilliant likeness but it was good enough to recognize his own face staring back at him.

He crumpled the paper and pocketed it before silently ushering the confused girl out of the shop.

'What's wrong? What was written on that piece of paper?'

'It was a picture of me. I guess those guys have been looking for me ever since that night. Look, we have to separate fast. Does that guy in there know you, the cashier I mean?'

'I don't think so, at least not where I live. I don't go in there that often and I've never seen him anywhere else.'

'OK, let's hope he doesn't know you. He definitely doesn't know me. Look… Sorry what is your name?'

'Holly, Holly Winters. What's yours?'

'I don't think you should know my name, it might not be safe for either of us. Tell you what I'll do,' he answered, reaching inside his hold-all to grab a pen. 'I'll write my phone number on your arm. When you get home copy it somewhere safe and then wash your arm clean. If you think someone may be following you or watching your house, give me a call and I'll come running. Apart from that I don't think we should ever meet again and I'd stay out of that shop for at least a year.'

'OK, if you think that's best.' She looked a little crestfallen. 'I really am sorry about what happened that night. I don't know how to say thank you; they could've done anything to me if you…'

'That's OK, Holly. Now get moving and don't go attacking any more cars.' He turned and sped away.

Holly scuffed her shoe against the ground and muttered quietly, 'Bet he wouldn't have disappeared so fast if I was older,' before running off in the opposite direction.

It took another two days for one of Cossanti's informers to identify Holly from the store's security pictures of her and Luke. On the third evening, as she was returning home, she spotted the shiny limo parked among all the beat-up autos along from her apartment block. She turned around and walked back until she could slip into a side alley and start running. She ran as fast as she could to reach the rear fire-escape and climb the stairs two at a time until she reached her floor. Half a minute later she was talking to Luke on her cell phone, explaining what she had seen and why she was calling.

'That's OK, Holly, but get out of there now in case they saw you climbing in the back window. Get your family out as well.'

'I got no family except my sister and she's still at work.'

'OK, you get out right now. I'll meet you a few blocks away; by the bus station, that's a nice busy place. They won't try anything there even if they do follow you. Trust me kid; I'll be there in a few minutes. Oh, and my name's Luke; I don't think it matters any more whether you know it or not.'

It didn't matter but Holly sounded thrilled to have a name to put to her mysterious hero. 'I'll be there Luke,' she answered as if in a trance. 'I won't let you down, I promise.'

She was still in a day-dream when someone grabbed her from behind and bundled her into the limo as she left the alley. She couldn't scream because her assailant's hand covered her mouth and when she tried to bite him he knocked her senseless with one blow from his other hand.

Luke waited for twenty minutes at the bus station growing more anxious every moment but there was still no sign of Holly. He wasn't surprised when the call came from Cossanti. He'd already guessed they were holding her as hostage for him.

'If you want the kid to stay alive, you get here, punk. You and me, we got a little business to settle and then we all go our separate ways. I said when we first met: you mess with me, you're messing with fire. Well, now you're going to find out what that means,' Cossanti said, barely able to conceal his malevolent joy at finally reaching the man who had humiliated and disfigured him.

He wanted to gloat about what he was going to do to Luke and how he was going to kill him slowly, but then he might have abandoned the girl and fled, so he kept that quiet. 'And don't go calling the cops. I got friends there, and they'll call me the moment you try to get some help,' he added, closing that possible escape route.

'Ok, Cossanti, you win this time. I'll walk to the back of the bus station, you can pick me up there. Don't go harming the girl though. I'd hate for you to regret it later.' Luke ended the call and strolled a little too casually towards the rendezvous point. He was almost there when he knelt to re-tie his shoe lace — was it a co-incidence that on the other side of the road, another man in a smart suit was doing exactly the same?

Minutes later Luke climbed into that same limousine and it sped away while the door was still closing. On the back seat beside Luke sat Gus, holding a terrified Holly close against his chest with one hand; the other hand held a knife just inches from her throat. Next to the driver, a passenger, sitting half sideways and resting one arm on the back of his seat, pointed his silenced automatic straight at Luke. 'This is to make sure you behave, kid; we don't want any of that Kung-Fu shit on the way.'

'No problem, guys. We'll have a nice quiet drive out to see your boss. Besides, I don't use Kung-Fu,' Luke replied easily, while his mind sped into top gear, racing to assess the chances of overpowering the other men and, most important of all — how. Seconds later he gave a gasp and shouted, 'Look out for that cop!'

Sheer instinct took over; both passengers and the driver looked for the unseen threat. At once, Luke threw a fatal throat-crushing chop at Gus and simultaneously twisted the front passenger's arm and the automatic downwards. The passenger fired one shot harmlessly into the floor of the limo before Luke's other hand grasped the weapon and continued twisting until it pointed straight and level at the heart of the man holding it. Luke saw the fear spreading across the man's face as he realized what was going to happen, milliseconds before the weapon fired.

The driver could do nothing to help his accomplices except keep the limo steady. He sat absolutely still when the hot point of the silencer pressed against the back of his neck. His hands shook with fear, and he looked terrified about what might happen next — he might even have been grateful that he wasn't as dead as his companions.

'Pull over to the sidewalk and wait,' said Luke. 'And make sure that's a nice smooth stop, otherwise I might have to drive.'

The limo had barely stopped at the curb when a second vehicle pulled in across its nose, a third hemmed it in from behind, and a flurry of armed men surrounded it.

Luke smiled and gave a thumbs-up signal to the man standing nearest him, before ordering Holly to leave the limo. 'Get in the car behind, Holly, you'll be safe with them — they're FBI agents. I'll call and see you later — after I've had a word with Cossanti. I need to make sure he's not going to cause us any more problems.'

Holly wanted to move but the message to her legs wasn't getting through; she could only give Luke a big silly grin and say, 'You're fantastic… Amazing… So easy.'

'That's OK, Holly, but we have to keep moving. C'mon now, climb over that fat slob and go with those guys out there.' He was still speaking when the door opened and one of the agents reached in to drag Holly away.

As the agent pulled Holly clear, Luke ordered, 'Take her home and guard the place till I get there. The second car can follow but not too close.'

The agent carried Holly to the front car and bundled her into the back seat. Everything that had happened, the whole thing, was just too much for her to take in. Her heart raced close to bursting point because her dream man had rescued her a second time. Not only that; he was giving orders to FBI agents and they were doing what he said. All she could think of was how old he might be by the time she was old enough to marry him.

After that car sped away to take Holly home, Luke tapped the driver's neck with the automatic. 'Drive to Cossanti's place.'

Twenty minutes later, they arrived at the gates of an impressive mansion surrounded by a high stone wall. 'Put the window down, and signal the guard to open the gates,' Luke ordered. They opened after a second or two and the limo slid forward enough for Luke to fire and stop the guard ever operating the gate again.

'Up to the house; nice and easy as if nothing is wrong. If you get this right you might be one of the lucky ones who live long enough to tell his children about the day Mike Cossanti met his match.'

The wheels of the limo crunched over the shingle drive and up to the house. Cossanti stood licking his lips in anticipation at the top of a short wide set of steps. He looked like a spoilt child at Christmas who couldn't wait to mutilate his new toy. 'What took so long?' he called, peering into the darkened limo windows.

The smile vanished from his face as Luke stepped out on the far side of the limo. 'Hey Mike, it's great to see you again. Couple of your boys, they got tired on the way here – dead tired as a matter of fact. Poor old Gus, he always was a bit slow on the hand-to-hand stuff.'

'You son-of-a-bitch, you killed Gus?'

'Yeah, 'fraid so Mike, but don't feel sorry for him. Me, I pity the poor bastards who will have to carry the coffin. I think I just put out that fire you were talking about.' Luke answered without moving.

Cossanti had no idea what had happened but he knew everything had screwed up. He couldn't even reach for his revolver, as Luke was pointing the automatic straight at him.

He watched Luke move to one side of the limo and walk purposely towards him and with each step that he took, Mike's heart pounded faster. He couldn't decide whether Luke was going to arrest him or execute him. In desperation, Mike looked towards the sky, hoping he was going to be saved by the men in the helicopters buzzing around the building, or the police arriving with their sirens blaring.

It took a while, but eventually the FBI were satisfied that the local police had everything under control and most of their men left, either in cars or helicopters. A few waited until the police captain left, with Cossanti handcuffed and escorted by a pair of detectives.

'I really appreciate the help today,' Luke said, shaking the hands of the remaining agents. 'Hopefully one of my teams will return the favor just as fast, if the need ever arises.'

'You're welcome, Captain,' the senior agent replied. 'It was great to help rescue the girl and bring that crook to justice. I don't think he'll be tasting freedom for a very long time to come. Now, can we give you a ride back to town?'

'Well, the limo's kinda messy, so I'll take that offer. I guess I'd better go to the girl's place as I owe them an explanation.'

Back at the apartment, a few more FBI agents checked Luke's ID before allowing him to enter Holly's home. Inside, she was going wild with excitement; she threw herself at Luke to welcome him back as her superhero, astounded by his safe return. One of the agents had told her they had arrested Cossanti, but nothing else.

Holly's sister, Maddie, showed more restraint. She couldn't believe what he had done to save her sister. A mixture of fear and relief brought tears to her eyes.

Luke stepped closer to wipe them away with his thumbs. 'I'm sorry, I didn't mean to put you both out like this. I just thought I should call and explain what happened. Cossanti's under arrest now and there's nothing more to worry about. I'd love to take you out somewhere to celebrate but it's kinda late for Holly. Maybe another time… or… or we can just say goodbye if you prefer?'

'No, no we have to celebrate, don't we, Maddie?' Holly asked her sister, nodding her head slightly and pleading with her eyes.

Maddie seemed totally thrown by the question but she didn't say no. Instead, she looked across to Luke as if he might offer some acceptable solution.

Luke hesitated for a moment before suggesting the first idea that entered his head. 'How about we all go to the zoo tomorrow? We could see some animals and have lunch there; my treat for the three of us?'

'You don't have to treat me,' Maddie answered. 'It wasn't me you saved or rescued. Try to think of something else for the two of you.'

'I think that would be a bit odd,' Luke answered a little more confidently. 'I mean, I don't think I should take Holly out on my own. It's not like we're family or anything. Why don't you come as chaperone? It wouldn't be the same without you.'

'Please come, Maddie,' Holly begged, desperate not to lose contact with Luke. 'I'll do the dishes for the next week; two weeks. Just say yes.'

Luke could sense Maddie was weakening when she replied rather lamely, 'I'm not sure we should ruin your weekend. Do you really want to waste your day with us?'

In contrast, he had regained every ounce of his confidence. He gave Holly a wide grin. 'Absolutely. I'm sure Holly will love it and I expect we'll enjoy it as well.'

With no reason to stay any longer, Luke said goodbye and left, after shaking hands with both Holly and Maddie. The last agents left with him and gave him a ride home. On the way there, he couldn't help noticing the faint hint of perfume lingering on his hand and he wondered which of the two had been wearing it. What he couldn't understand was why that fragrance sent a few tingling shivers up and down his spine; even if he did know why, he wasn't going to admit it, not even to himself.

The next day, Luke was almost ready to meet the girls when his cell rang and he recognized the strained voice of the police captain. 'Sorry to bother you on a Saturday, but we need some more information on that first incident, when Cossanti threatened the girl with a knife. If it's OK with you, I'll get a couple of my guys to pick you up. Show them exactly where it happened, will you, and tell them anything else that you can remember? My guys are on their way over to you with the girl and her sister. This shouldn't delay your trip to the zoo more than ten or fifteen minutes.'

There didn't seem to be any point in refusing, so Luke confirmed he would be ready when they arrived. He left the house the moment he saw the car pulling up and headed for the rear passenger door. One of the detectives on board jumped out to give him a cheery greeting and hold the door open for him.

The girls' terrified looks startled Luke; a fraction too late, he realised that something was wrong. Then the world went black as the 'officer' brought the butt of his automatic down hard on Luke's head. He remained unconscious for the rest of the journey.

When he finally came round, his arms and legs were tied to the legs and back of a solid, old-fashioned wooden chair. It had a padded seat and back, with wooden bars between each leg that gave it a lot more strength, and heavy back legs that reached up in a smooth curve to form the chair back. Many years earlier it might have graced someone's dining room, but it had long since been consigned to the factory floor.

In this case, the factory floor was a long timber store with wooden slatted walls and a high roof of corrugated iron. At their end of the building were a few offices but Luke couldn't see any more than that.

'Yeah, the punk's finally back in the real world,' he heard Cossanti call through the confused mist of his throbbing head. 'This is the last time I'm telling you, punk, you mess with me, you're messing with fire. I even told you I had connections in the police but ya didn't believe me, ya little shit, did ya?'

Struggling to clear his head, Luke looked up and saw the police captain holding on to the ropes that tied Holly and Maddie together. His two officers stood behind Cossanti, grinning triumphantly, and he cursed his stupidity for ignoring the warning.

'It's not over, Cossanti. You haven't won yet. I don't think you've got the brains to win,' Luke struggled to say, knowing they were probably all about to die in a hail of bullets. He only spotted the aluminium baseball bat in Cossanti's hand after he finished speaking; this was going to be a lot more painful than a few fast bullets.

'Talk's cheap, punk. Let's hear what ya have to say when I start beating these two friends of yours.'

'Sure, go ahead Mike, I guess even you can beat up a girl and her kid sister. Maybe you're afraid I can still beat you with both hands tied to this chair?' Luke tried desperately to draw Mike's attention away from the girls; he was also trying to force the joints of the chair apart but, despite their age, each of the glued joints was holding firm.

'Why not? I been looking forward to this moment for a long time. Let's hear you begging to die before I put a bullet through their heads,' Cossanti replied, stepping closer to Luke.

As he raised the bat, one of the detectives couldn't stop himself from yelling out, 'Yeah, bust his head, Mr Cossanti, he ruined our whole setup in this town.'

Cossanti's face turned to thunder in an instant as he spun round to face the man. 'I decide what to do. You ever tell me what to do again, I'll reshape that stupid head of yours as well. Go get the lamp and the paraffin. Well, go on, both of ya, get out of here,' he shouted, waving the bat in their direction. After watching them disappear outside he turned his attention back to Luke; unfortunately for him, Luke now had a plan.

Luke continued baiting Cossanti, building on the anger he had already shown to the detectives. 'You're losing control, Cossanti. You should quit before they turn on you.' By the time the thug raised the bat again, he looked determined to crush Luke's skull with the first blow. As the bat started downwards, Luke pressed his toes against the concrete floor, tipping the chair backwards and leaving the blow to strike the wooden bars below the seat.

With even greater fury, Cossanti raised the bat again and screamed at Luke as he brought it down a second time. Luke dodged the blow by throwing his weight to one side and tipping the chair sideways. When that blow missed, it broke the remaining bars and Cossanti went berserk. He stepped closer and raised the bat to its maximum height before bringing it down as hard as he could.

Cossanti was no baseball player and definitely no golfer. Instead of concentrating on the ball, he put all his effort into the stroke. When the bat reached where Luke should have been lying, he was no longer there. With greater freedom to move, he span sideways and onto his front, leaving the solid back legs to take the impact.

What should have been a painless follow-through came to a bone-shuddering stop, like a golfer hitting a tree instead of the ball. Both chair legs broke on impact but so did one of Cossanti's wrists; he dropped the bat as if it were red hot.

Without the strength of the bars or the back legs, the chair surrendered its prisoner the instant Luke stretched out his limbs. Everything happened in a blur after that. Cossanti tried to draw his revolver but dropped it on the floor instead. The police captain fired two shots at Luke before he ducked to avoid the bat that Luke threw at him. When he tried to take a third shot, he died in the return fire after Luke dived to retrieve Cossanti's weapon. The two returning detectives fired at Luke as they ran towards him, forcing him to slither along the floor to a better vantage point. One detective died in the return fire and the second tried to flee but crashed down before he had taken three more steps.

Luke rested for no more than a second before twisting around to prevent Cossanti attacking him again. All he could see was the dead police captain and the two girls struggling with the ropes around their waists.

'Where's Cossanti?' Luke asked as he helped free the girls.

'He went through that office door, but don't follow him. He might have another gun or something. Let's get out of here the way we came in,' Maddie replied, grabbing Luke's arm to stop him following Cossanti.

One glance convinced them it wasn't possible to leave by that route. The lighted lamp that the second detective had been carrying had smashed on the floor and ignited the paraffin in its plastic container. The fire had spread to the wood shavings beside the door and the whole area was fast becoming an inferno.

'We have to follow Cossanti. Keep behind me, but not too close, in case he does have another weapon,' Luke said, pulling the mesmerized Holly along.

They ran through the first office and then a second before climbing three flights of stairs. At the top, an outside door led to the fire escape. They were halfway down before Luke realised the bottom gate was locked shut and barbed wire covered the side railing. That escape route was blocked.

'We have to go up; it's the only way. There has to be another way down from the top,' Luke called out, leading the way further up the stairs. At the top, he cautiously poked his head over the parapet and then bounded onto the tin roof. Fifty feet ahead of him, Cossanti was struggling to climb a metal ladder onto the next roof; with only one usable hand, it was proving impossible.

Luke made it even harder by firing a shot at the good hand. Cossanti collapsed, writhing in agony, before the sound of the shot had died away. He rolled over a few times and struggled back to his feet.

'It's time to surrender, Mike. There's no way you can escape now and all your police friends are dead.'

Cossanti continued to back further away.

'No, I won't do it. I'll make it out, and then I'll come back for you. No matter how long it takes, I'll always come back to get you.'

Luke finally accepted there was only one sure way to finish with Cossanti. He ordered the girls to climb the ladder. Once they were safely on their way, he followed the retreating figure of Cossanti into the swirling smoke.

Luke followed him along the roof for another hundred feet or so, inching forward and struggling to see. Suddenly the raging fire below them exploded through the glass skylights a few feet in front of him, leaving no way of getting past the searing heat and flames.

In combat Luke had never retreated but this time there was no choice; he either burned or turned as the smoke and flames soared into the sky. Back at the ladder he could hear the girls yelling for him to hurry over the growing roar of the fire. As he climbed frantically towards them, he wondered whether it was too late to escape; his hands could barely grasp the hot metal steps and he felt the scorching heat of the flames closing in behind him.

'Go,' he begged the girls. 'Get out of here, don't wait for me. Please, for God's sake, run.' Despite his constant demands that they leave, they waited until they had pulled him the last few feet to safety and then staggered in the choking smoke towards the next building and safety. Each roof they crossed needed either another ladder to reach, or a small wall to climb over and they never stopped running until they reached the last one. Only then did they look back to see Cossanti, trapped like a rat and frantic to escape from the last section of his roof.

Maddie started crying, cupping her face in her hands. 'Oh God, that could have been us dying in that fire if you hadn't saved us again. I don't think we can ever repay you. Not with money, not with anything.'

Luke stepped a little closer to Maddie and gently eased her hands away from her face. 'I'll settle for a kiss if that's OK with you? Just a little one in case you don't like it.'

Maddie didn't answer, she just smiled briefly and leant ever so slightly towards Luke and tipped her chin a fraction higher. He only meant the kiss to last a moment but when neither of them tried to end it, Luke released his grip on her hands to grasp her tight in his arms.

Holly's dreams and fantasies about Luke evaporated in a split second as she watched them holding on to each other as if their lives depended on it.

'I bet he's got bad breath,' she mumbled angrily but then changed her mind just as quickly; she didn't like the idea of a brother-in-law with that problem.

She turned her attention back to the fire and watched Cossanti jumping up and down on the glowing roof in a futile attempt to stop the searing metal burning his feet. She turned again to try and interrupt the passionate embrace, so she missed the final sight of Cossanti falling into the inferno when the roof collapsed.

She couldn't resist saying, 'You remember Cossanti said we were messing with fire if we messed with him? Well, we messed with him and now he's dancing with fire.'

ON TINTOCK TAP

GARY BONN

'WHEN WE GET TO THE TOP I can wave to mum and dad. It's like saying goodb… hello. I think we'll see Glasgow, don't you?' Ben asks. On the other side of the burn, Morag sits, looking down and swishing her feet in the stream. Still in trainers. Mud and dark stains wash from them. She doesn't speak. He goes on. 'Did you tell your mum we were coming up here?'

Morag tenses, looks up and nods.

'Well, did you?'

'I tried to. There were so many flies. I was scared.'

'In the kitchen?'

'Yes. I think she's still asleep, like dad.'

'Where's he?'

Morag looks down the hill, narrows her eyes and points. 'That field. I didn't want to go in because of the dogs.'

'Your dogs?'

'No. I don't know where they came from. They scared me yesterday. I think they're still there. Did you see Mrs… Your foster… Um, Abbey and Chris to say goodbye?'

'No. I don't know where they've gone. Their car's gone too. I don't know if they were looking for me. I don't know when they'll be back. Abbey was sick a lot. Maybe they went to the doctor.' Ben looks up the path. Steep and rocky, gored in places by the hooves of sheep and grooved by water, it looks forbidding. 'How much longer do we have to keep going up?'

'I don't know. Dad carried me on his shoulders last time. It was fun and he sang songs.' She leans forward. 'I want to put my hands in the water too, they hurt.' She looks at Ben. 'It's not like I'm drinking it.'

'But how high is the mountain?' Ben asks.

'As high as high can be.'

'Do we have to go to the top?'

'Right to the top. There's lots of rocks there. Mum and dad said that's where the magic is; at the very, very top.'

Ben stifles a sob. 'But it's so big. If only it was flatter; it would be easy.'

'Don't you have mountains in Glasgow?'

'No, silly. There's no room.'

Morag closes her eyes as the cold water soothes her hands. 'Do you think it would be bad to put my face in? It hurts too.'

Ben shakes his head. 'That's nearly drinking it. All the badness will get into you and you'll…' He founders over the next word.

'But I'm so thirsty.' Morag stands and winces, moving her weight from one foot to the other. 'Come on.' She looks down at Ben. 'Get up. *Come on!*'

'It's so hard… We've been walking for ages and ages.' Ben's eyes fill with tears.

'Ben, I can't go up alone. I'm scared and you're a boy. You're supposed to be strong. And you're nearly a year older than me… and everything.'

'When are you six?' asks Ben, reaching for a heather root on which to pull himself up. He stops and tries not to look at his hand.

'Tomorrow. I *think* it's tomorrow. Come on, Ben. I can't pull you up because of my skin.'

Morag stumbles at the top of the bank. A tiny slip, she lands on her side and screams with the pain of it. Ben shuffles, tries not to look, knows he can't help her up without both of them suffering as a result. Reaches out, wanting to take her hand, steps back again, arms at his sides.

Whimpering from a screwed up mouth, Morag gets to her feet. 'Ben, this is so sore. Nothing should be so sore.'

They stand looking into each other's eyes. Eyes tortured with pain and unspoken fear. Morag's breathing settles; she looks up the hill. 'Not far, not far.' She points. 'The path goes between the rocky bits. The magic place is behind a wall.'

'Morag,' Ben stifles another sob, 'that's very far. It's very steep.'

She turns on him and screeches, 'What else is there to do? What else; what else; *what else?*'

'Stop shouting!' Ben leans forward hands over his ears, eyes tight closed.

Morag limps forward, up the path. 'Well I'm going. Someone's got to make everything better.'

Ben can't answer. To do so would burst the dam holding back the unspeakable. A pact they've made without realising it: a way to cope. He stumbles on behind her.

The path steepens. Firm red soil holds just enough water to make Morag's trainers grip. As she moves she recites, 'On Tintock tap there is a *mist*.' Her next step taken every time she says the last word.

'What's a Tintock?' mutters Ben.

She doesn't answer, lost in her chant.

'What's a Tintock?' Ben shouts this time, staggering among heather shoots.

'Ssh. I'm making the mist.'

'What are you on about?'

'This is Tinto, this mountain. It used to be called Tintock. That's its magic name.'

'Does it have a tap? I'm so thirsty.'

'Tap means top. But there is a cup there.'

'With water that we can really drink?'

'Just one drop. We'll share it.'

'Just one drop?'

'It's magic.'

'You say that about everything. I don't believe you.' Ben stops and stands, swaying. 'I'm staying here. This is stupid.'

'You can't stop. *You mustn't.*'

Ben sits down, arms on knees and rests his head. 'I'm not going.'

'Ben…?'

'No.'

'It's not far.'

'Go away.'

Morag turns. Too dehydrated to cry, her eyes sting. 'On Tintock tap there is a mist. On Tintock tap there is a mist…'

Ben raises his head when he hears her shrieks cracking with despair. He rises and, lips pressed in a grim line of pain, heads towards the noise. 'I'm coming!' he shouts.

'Ben, Ben. We've gone the wrong way. I can't find the stile,' Morag sobs, pulling a bare arm over her eyes.

Blood on her hands and the ragged rocks of the dry-stone wall she's been trying to climb.

'I'll help you over the wall. No, look the stile's over there.'

'Where? I can't see it. It's all a bit grey. Is the mist coming down?'

Ben, with a flash of wisdom far beyond his years, doesn't mention that there's no mist. His own eyesight's fading too. 'Here, I won't hold your hand. I'll hold your shoulder.'

'Have I done something very bad to my hands? I have, haven't I? Like when I fell. I think some of my skin tore.'

'You're fine.' Revelation breaks through Ben's resistance. He sees the truth of things, a shock: a strange relief with it. He feels dizzy with responsibility, elation that he can meet it. He'll get Morag to where she wants to go and then look after her. Strength comes to him. The strength that goes with knowing you've nothing left to save it for. They get to the stile and he climbs it, leaden legs shaking.

'One more step up. There's a thick bit to stand on.' Ben looks at the flesh hanging from Morag's hands. 'You don't need to touch the rail; just come forward.'

The sun comes out and Morag says she can see a bit better.

Ben makes sure she's safely off the stile and turns to the cairn on the summit. 'You're right, Morag. It's not far, really close. It's all rocks in a bit. I'll put my arm round you.'

Morag asks, 'Can you see the kist?'

'The what?'

'It means chest. A thing you put things in.' Morag's words rasp in her throat. She stops and shudders, her stomach heaving.

'You all right? You feeling sick?'

'I've felt sick for days. It's getting worse.'

'Me too. Come on. We'll go really slow. One bit at a time.'

'Can you see the kist?'

'I'll look for it.'

Morag chants, 'And in that mist there is a kist. And in that mist there is a kist.' To Ben she says, 'I'm making the kist.' She stumbles and stops. 'Can I sit yet?'

'Just a few steps and we're as high as can be. All the magic will be there.' Despite their fragile flesh, Ben catches her as she stumbles again. They both squeal as raw nerves tear and burn. 'Here, we can stop. Don't cry. We can sit down now,' he says. 'Turn round. There's a flat stone. It's big enough for both of us.'

Through her sobs, she says, 'You *are* strong and brave. Can you see the kist?'

Ben's mind races. 'It's here. I can feel it. But you have to believe in it.' He pauses. 'I know it's sore, but can I take your hand? I can guide it. We'll both open the kist.' He moves her hand; she stiffens and gasps. 'It won't hurt for long. The magic will help us. Can you feel the kist just here?'

'No.'

'Believe you can feel it. Believe it.'

'I can't...'

'What's it made of?'

'I don't...'

'Feel it.'

'Wood; it's wood.'

'Here's the catch. We can open it now. Can you hear the lid? It's creaking.'

'Yes.' The faintest whimper from Morag. 'Can you see the cup?'

'A cup? Yes. It's an old brown one like my nana has in her house. Let's lift it. Open your mouth.'

'I can't see it, Ben. Has the sun gone down already?'

Ben feels his heart break. The sun's touching the low hills on his right. 'It's the mist getting thick.'

'It's getting colder too.'

'Take a sip. What does it taste like?'

'Will you drink some too?'

'After you.' He watches her drink from the imaginary cup, her swollen tongue running over cracked and scabbed lips.

'It's lovely...' A flake of dried blood falls from the corner of her mouth.

Ben pretends to drink too, stops himself, forces the dream into his mind, into his mouth. Tastes the water, feels it's coolness. 'That's the best drop of water ever.'

'I liked it when you had your arm round me. Will you do it again?'

'I'll try not to hurt you.'

Morag presses close, experimentally, bit by bit against the pain. 'When we grow up, we'll have to get married.'

'What?'

'Cos, we're the only ones left, aren't we?'

So, at last, the dam bursts. The words can flood out.

Ben says, 'I think everyone's dead. No one's going to come.'

'But how will we pay bills and things? I don't know how.'

'There won't be bills.'

'Why?'

'There were missiles. Now it's satellites and stuff. They're burning everything. They burned Glasgow.'

'Like they did to other places far, far away over the sea? Like on telly?'

'Chris said they're out of control. He says the people who made them are dead. The satellites broke a power station and badness got out. The missiles made badness too. It gets into the air and comes down in the rain and gets into all our water. The satellites make things hot. They made those huge clouds that dropped all the ice that broke the roofs and killed people at Jordan's farm.'

'But why? Why do they do that?'

'Chris said it was a war. It happened so fast they didn't have time to tell anyone.'

Morag looks up. 'I can see magic now. Dancing lights like fairies. It's very faint. It's lovely.'

To the south, across the Southern Uplands, erupts a vast electrical storm reaching to the horizons. Ben wonders if the satellites are moving down the country all the time and who'll be left when they've finished. The storm's thundering roar reaches and shakes them, makes speech impossible. They sit, shivering until they can speak again.

'What will it be like when we're married? Can we have two dogs for the sheep? Mum says three make too much mess.'

'I like dogs. We weren't allowed any in our flat.'

'That was a lovely drink, but I'm still a *bit* thirsty.'

'We'll have some more in a minute.'

Morag whispers,

'On Tintock tap there is a mist

And in that mist there is a kist

And in that kist there is a cup

And in that cup there is a drap

Tak up the cup and drink that drap that's in yon kist on Tintock tap.'

She stops and wheezes. 'Ben…' she starts, chokes and goes on. 'My feet and hands don't hurt now. The magic's working. It's getting harder to talk. I'm so sleepy.'

Ben feels his own feet growing numb and lifeless — an improvement on the burning pain of the last day. He'd been too scared to take his shoes off in case he couldn't cope with what they revealed. Frost glitters among the laces. He cuddles Morag for a while and watches the stars come out. The moon sends soft light down, silvering Morag's hair. A group of three satellites, with petals like flowers and looking almost as big as the moon, flash as they catch the sun. They rotate as a group, a slow waltz of death, and fade into the earth's shadow.

'Hey, you,' Ben says, looking down at Morag. 'I don't think you should sleep with your eyes open. I'll help you close them. I'll be ever so gentle.'

The moon and stars track slowly across the sky. His free arm is too numb to lift, so he can't see his watch.

'I think I need to doze for a bit. It's very late. Sleep well, Morag.'

'Upa 'upa (The Firedance)

Bill Sauer and Lillian Reyes

5 August, 1889

My Dearest Charlotte Rae,

My guilt-ridden heart begs forgiveness; my apologies for allowing too much time to pass in our correspondence. I pledge to rectify my tardiness from this letter forward, this being writ on the eve of my departure for Tahiti. On the morrow, I shall be standing on the deck of the barkentine *City of Papeete* as she departs San Francisco harbor. I'm to do as I set out to do so long ago, dear sister. My tropical adventure begins now.

The muse calls, Charlotte, and I simply cannot resist her pull. Farther and farther west I have travelled since leaving Georgia, until I reached the coast. Now the sea beckons, and the mysteries she hides on her island jewels. I assure you, though (and you may provide comfort to Mama, as well), that this is not an entirely frivolous endeavor. This past March, the editor of San Francisco's *The Morning Call* did commission me to provide a series of articles chronicling my time in the tropical paradise, along with regular reportage on life, trade and politics there. My assignment is Tahiti in particular, as the French ambassador there has been making noises alluding toward the acquisition of a direct steamship route from San Francisco to those islands, and back. As well, the *Los Angeles Daily Herald* and *Sacramento Daily Record-Union* already print "special correspondence" from the South Seas, so my editor wishes to follow suit. He is particularly interested in gaining my perspective as an ex-Confederate, though I fail to see the pertinence in this day and age.

My departure has been delayed some months due to fears of weather, after the horrible aftermath of the storm upon Samoa in March of

'UPA 'UPA (THE FIREDANCE)

this year. I'm told the passage to Tahiti will take between thirty-five and forty days, weather contingent. Although I've never spent so much time in the confinement of a seagoing vessel, I'm sure it can be no worse than my stay at that place of which we do not speak. In fact, my memories of that hellish place will bring me comfort, by comparison, should I begin to feel low. Even thoughts of that stink-hole of a cave in Northern Virginia may serve to give me perspective. A month on a sailing ship could be no worse, I imagine.

Oh Charlotte, I do miss you terrible, but I must complete this journey. Robert Louis Stevenson departed this very same port for the Marquesas just one year ago, and I long to follow his path now. I delayed too long any endeavor in discovering my worth as a man beyond Mama's expectations of me. The machinations she thrust upon you and your own beloved Robert, this was the catalyst to my enlightenment. I am still heartbroken for you, and though you seem to have made your peace with her, I cannot forgive so easily on your behalf.

I can only hope to someday find a woman to love me as you did your Robert, one for whom the hideousness of my visage is rendered invisible by her adoration for me. Even in the golden cities of California, ladies turn away or stare rudely at my scar, no different from home. Perhaps the French Colonists or British missionaries of Papeete will be more accepting of my disfigurement.

But enough of my laments. Look at me going on endlessly, as if I have been in misery! Believe me Charlotte, I have not. I apologize if I give the impression of such nonsense. Please tell Mama I am well and she need not fret for me. The package accompanying this letter contains gifts for both of you: Genuine kid gloves of the 12-button length, imported by the renowned Newman and Levinson of San Francisco. Think of me well when you wear them, and write to me quickly. I have enclosed the name and address of my editor. He will forward any correspondence to me.

Be well, dear Charlotte.

Tobias

October 22, 1889

My dearest brother,

It was with great felicity that I received your letter today. It has been too long since you wrote — last I heard you were having quite the time up north in the "windy city", though it did surprise me that you would ever return there. Truly, I have been eagerly awaiting your word but do not burden yourself over my worries. Now I know you are alive and well and all is right in the world.

I am fine, as is Mama. She complains of the gout more each day; how it pains her. Old Dr. Martin visited the other day and he regrets there is nothing to be done except make her comfortable.

Though I know you are out exploring the new and barely discovered world, I wish with all my heart you were still in Savannah with us. Autumn and all her colorful glory are slowly departing as creep in the cold, dreary months of winter. As you well know, this has always been my favorite time of year. The last of the gold and brown leaves have fallen and the trees stand stark and bare against a crisp blue sky. To me, the air smells fresher; the whole world seems cleaner. If we're lucky, a bit of snow might fall this winter but even without that wintery treat, I still delight to sit in the parlor by the warmth of our little hearth. I can't yet think of Christmas; it will be our first one apart since the war. Do you remember when we were children, how majestic our big old manor house looked? With the boughs of holly and mistletoe hanging everywhere and how father would take us out to select just the perfect tree to bring home? Ah, those were rich times, before the war. It seems so far away now, another lifetime; yet I guard them close to my heart to warm me like the hearth fire.

Oh dear brother, I miss you so! Now more than ever. As does Mama, though she'd never say as much. You know it is her nature to keep her own counsel and this makes her of a reserved disposition. Now you are so far away and our only correspondence these written words; it recalls to us those unpleasant years during the War of Northern Aggression. How we worried for you then and our anxiety is not lessened for the passage of time.

'Upa 'upa (The Firedance)

As to Mama, she has lost so much in her life already. First Rufus to that awful cholera and then Papa in the War. And when we thought we'd lost you as well, she's just never been quite the same. Indeed, I found it in myself to forgive her. With the passing years, I've come to realize there is naught that matters more than family. It is in truth all that we have. Now, you and I are all that Mama has in this world. While I miss Robert terribly, perhaps Mama was right and it wasn't the most serendipitous match. Who could have thought that I, of all people, would fall madly in love with a bluecoat Yankee? I only lament that I am now an old maid and will live the rest of my days without a spouse or children of my own. I suppose all I have in this world is Mama. And you, sweet Tobias. Do please forgive our mother, I beg of you.

Oh, what grand adventures you must be having! Your descriptions of the golden coast from your newspaper clippings amazed me; I can scarce imagine a place so extraordinary. I await your descriptions of the even more exotic islands in Tahiti. I dare say your adventures are the only excitement I find these days.

I know you feel you must go searching for something you could not find here in Georgia. I, too, wish you to find a love that is good and strong. I have every confidence there is a woman existing on the Lord's earth for you. Do not fret over your advanced age; if a spinster such as myself could find a husband at the ripe age of nine and twenty, a man of your fine character will do just fine.

As to your scars, mayhap I am unduly influenced; however your face has always been precious to me. Surely any decent woman will look past such superficial marring to appreciate your handsomeness of form and beauty in spirit.

Oh! And the gloves you sent were absolutely gorgeous, just what I needed to complete my evening toilette. Mama and I will wear them this very winter and I know I will think of you fondly as I do so, though I cannot presume to speak for Mama. I eagerly await your next post. Until then, I remain always—

Your loving sister,

Charlotte Rae

24 December, 1889

My Dearest Charlotte Rae,

Your letter reached my eager hands and eyes today; for a finer Christmas gift, I could not ask. Yet it would be false witness were I not to give voice to my sadness over your seeming dismissal of true love's value. I read Mama's voice in your words, though I mean no disrespect by this. I cannot deny the importance of family, but I do lately question its worth above the preservation of self and sanity when family ties so strongly work against the same. I miss you terribly, Charlotte, but like my time away during the unpleasantness of the war, this distance is neither insurmountable nor of limitless duration. It will seem like no time at all before I will be giving you and Mama great big bear hugs again. Yes, Mama too. Time will bring me around, I'm sure of this truth.

Papeete is not as I expected. Though the crystal-blue sea and lush, green, living mountains of Tahiti surround her, Papeete is plain, nondescript in her architecture and the European dominance of her populace. My life here is already settling into a comfortable, all-too-familiar matter of course, though my passage proved much less so. A hurricane on the 23rd of August caught us in the ragged skirt hem of her fury. Not enough weather to turn us about, but duly enough to toss us violently like a child's bath toy. The captain insisted I not leave my cabin for three days and nights straight. Nonetheless, the reportage I produced did result in my first credit in *The Morning Call*, so the experience did not entirely lack benefit. Damage to the barkentine *City of Papeete* proved minimal, delaying our arrival by only two days.

I must confess that comfort is not my intent for this adventure. Papeete is foul with political and high-societal chicanery, in every way a gossip machine as prolific as our own Savannah. I could have daily reports piling up for my editor if I could stomach it, but I cannot. It does not allow me to miss the trappings of home at all, despite my want to see and speak to you again, dear Charlotte.

As such, an opportunity may be developing for me to make new residence near a native village, far from Papeete and deeper in the island's jungle. I will take it without hesitation should it come to fruition. A chance meeting with a pair of brothers native to the

'Upa 'upa (The Firedance)

island resulted in conversation leading to this possibility. It seems their particular tribe remains more of the warrior ilk than most of the island's original inhabitants, the majority becoming more and more "civilized" over time. These men view my facial disfigurement as the marks of a fellow warrior, of honor and tribute to a life lived bravely. They believe their elders will allow me to take up residence with an adoptive family among them until I prove my own worth. Not since my time as a Mosby Ranger have I felt so welcomed outside of my own home with you and Mama.

Rest assured that I would not lose all touch with the benefits of civilized living. I would still be visiting Papeete regularly to correspond with my editor, so letters from you will not be lost or wasted and mine to you shall never cease. You, dear sister, are a lifeline I must not sever, a tie to my civilized self I mustn't forget, no matter what changes the wilds of Tahiti may influence upon me. Do send me more news of home soon, no matter how trivial you may deem it. Yet, perhaps my news might influence you to seek adventure of your own, to disregard some of the lazy comforts of Savannah living so that you might again feel the glory all of creation has to offer you. I only wish the full depths of life's joy for you.

Be well, dear Charlotte,

Tobias

March 16, 1890

Dear, dear Tobias,

Your correspondence reached us just as Father Winter eased his icy cold grip on Savannah's bustling streets. Mama's health has been better in recent weeks; the warmer weather is of great help. We can feel spring's promise of new life slumbering just under the surface, waiting to burst out with all her vibrant colors.

I have no words adequate to express my relief at your safe arrival. Your description of the hurricane at sea gave Mama quite a fit of the vapors and I must admit I was not unaffected. I beg of you, have care brother mine, so that you may return safe again to your loving mother and sister.

Christmas came and went quietly this year, then the New Year snuck past like a thief in the night. I helped the ladies of the Daughters of the Confederacy put on quite the festive gathering this year and I believe the tree in Forsythe Park was the most beautiful it has ever been. Mama was unable to leave the house and I spent many nights seeking solace by the warmth of our hearth fire, reading an old favorite, "The Adventures of Robinson Crusoe". I find myself imagining you in the well-worn pages of that island adventure.

How lovely that you have encountered some civilization in mysterious Papeete. I know you consider it droll but it should keep you somewhat civilized during your time there. Your description of the island tests the limits of my imagination; it sounds much like paradise! Yet I shiver in trepidation at the thought of you venturing into the wilds of its jungle.

I am so pleased that you have found friends and acceptance, which is only what you deserve. However, do be careful! You say the majority of the natives are civilized but what do you really know of the uncivilized ones? Are they like the red Indians of the west? I remember when we went to that that "Wild West Show" in '82. Thank heavens Robert was with us — those Indians with their paint and screaming gave me quite a scare!

Oh, you make me want to see the world. I read your letters and think perhaps I shall pack up and head out to parts unknown. They are just girlish fantasy, of course, from a woman far too old to have them anymore. I shall consign myself to live vicariously through you.

'UPA 'UPA (THE FIREDANCE)

You are such a romantic spirit, Tobias; the passage of time and hardships has not changed that and I am grateful. You are correct in saying I have abandoned the notion of romantic love, as it has abandoned me. I am no longer the carefree innocent from our plantation in Charleston those many years ago. If my heart has hardened it is because the spirit does what it must. I give all of my heretofore-unrealized dreams and hopes of true love unto you, sweet brother.

Enclosed is a shirt I sewed for you, made of the softest seersucker fabric, which I hope will serve you well in the hotter climes of Tahiti. I know you have a terrible habit of staining your clothing with ink while writing and thought that surely you must be in want of a new one by now. I hope it covers you well until you can be wrapped in the bosom of your family again.

Love always, your sister,

Charlotte Rae

22 July, 1890

Dearest Charlotte,

What a fortunate surprise, to find your letter waiting for me upon my visit to Papeete this morning. As I write this reply, I sit upon the steps of a tiki hut, surrounded by the balmy waters of the Pacific, my bare feet cooling in its caresses. The sun dances golden atop the crystal waters as it slowly sinks into the sea; soon it will be candle-lighting and my writing will have to continue under the light of a full moon reflected off the indigo. I remain in Papeete for the evening as a guest of the French Ambassador, enjoying the hospitality of this private hut for my night's rest. I shall travel back to the other side of the island at morning's first light.

You may ask how a man such as myself might garner the attention of such a dignitary as the Ambassador. It seems he is an aficionado and collector of firearms. A common acquaintance mentioned to him my possession of a genuine Sharps carbine with sharpshooter's scope, the only relic I have allowed myself to keep from my time as a Mosby's Man during the war. His desire to see it earned me an invitation to dinner, and reluctant tales of my war experiences endear me to him. Lately he has embraced me as a means to further his campaign to institute several steamship routes directly to Tahiti. As it stands, steamships from the US coast come to Papeete by way of Hawaii; the only direct lines are still the slower sailing vessels. As long as my reportage mentions his desire every few weeks, and in doing so I place it in the most positive light possible, I enjoy an open invitation to the use of this hut and the ambassador's kitchen.

Speaking of the kitchen, I have encountered many exotic dishes you or I would never have dreamt of eating back in Savannah, as wonderful as the cuisine is there. One in particular I believe you would love as much as I do, dear Charlotte: *poisson cru*, as the French call it, or *e'ia ota* as my native friends do: uncooked red tuna in a marinade of lime or lemon juice (though I actually prefer a combination of both), tossed with some vegetables and coconut milk. Yes, Charlotte, uncooked, but it is divine in its creaminess and depth of flavor, despite the simplicity of preparation. I cannot get enough of it and

'UPA 'UPA (THE FIREDANCE)

fear I may need to double my morning runs through the jungle in order to counter its effects upon my midriff.

Ah, but I am remiss to go on about these things without returning to my brief mention of my current residence on the other side of the big island. Yes, Charlotte, the opportunity to live with an adoptive family was afforded me — in fact, shortly after writing you last, though it was not without trial, I must add. As a test of my mettle and willingness to trust my sponsors, it was required that I accompany them through the caves and tunnels created long ago by the volcano that birthed these islands.

For hours and hours through near pitch, the only light from a small torch held by the lead guide, I followed them. Sometimes the tunnels would narrow to mere tubes, barely large enough to crawl through, and my guides would not slow for me. In one of the narrowest passages, I lost sight of the light. In utter darkness, I had no choice but to inch forward on my belly despite my trepidation and the rawness of my knees, elbows and palms, the faint voices of my companions providing the only assurance I would ever see the sun again. It took me back to the tunnels my fellow prisoners dug beneath Camp Davis. This time, instead of armed Yankee guards greeting me at the end, I emerged to one of the most beautiful sights I have ever witnessed.

A mighty cavern opened before me, great inverted points of glistening stone seeming to flow down from somewhere above. We stood on a stone ledge, high above a shimmering tide pool, the eerie turquoise glow coming from sunlight through an underwater cave opening. The lead guide tossed the torch high into the air, and for a moment I could see just how high the ceiling above me went. The stone sparkled as if bejeweled with sapphire, ruby, garnet and jade, until the seawater extinguished the torch. One by one, my three guides leapt from our perch into the pool and disappeared beneath the surface as they swam through the opening. The fall matched the height of a four-story building, Charlotte! Having no heart to crawl back through the dark again, my only choice became clear and I followed them into the blue. To my shock, this water was much colder than I've become accustomed to; it reminded me more of a dip in the creek back home than a swim in the Pacific. Once my breath returned to me, I steeled my nerve and dove deep to the exit. To my pleasant surprise, the water became drastically warmer as I entered the sunlight and I found myself in a lagoon on the opposite side of the island from which we had embarked.

On the shore, my guides whooped and hollered as my head broke the water's surface. Much like those "Scouts of the Prairie" Indians who gave you that scare, but these were happy sounds, and sincere in their delivery. I had passed their test and have lived near Mataiea at the southern end of the big island ever since, far from Papeete to the north. My adoptive family is very kind, though they keep me busy. I've become a very adept fisherman, and have even learned to dive for pearls! This leads me to the gifts I'm including with this letter. Enclosed, for you and Mama both, are a few genuine black pearls that I have personally harvested from the lagoon of Rangiroa, a smaller island to the north of Tahiti. A reputable jeweler will be able to set them in any way you desire. I imagine you'll be the talk of the town, displaying your rare black pearls at the latest society event.

Well, dear Charlotte, as another exhausting yet glorious day ends on my tropical paradise, so must I end this letter. As has been my practice of late, I have enclosed a second letter written earlier, one which you may safely read aloud to Mama without worry of upsetting her. Nonetheless, I have the greater portion of a day's paddling to make my way back to my new home. I do all of my travelling on foot or in a canoe now. I do miss the companionship of my horses, but so much walking and rowing keeps me in better health than I have known since I was a very young man. Someday I will find a way to bring you here, Charlotte; it would do a world of wonders for you.

Until then, I remain your loving brother,

Tobias

'Upa 'upa (The Firedance)

November 12, 1890

Dear Tobias,

How joyful is the day when I receive one of your letters. Nothing puts me in better spirits. I worry about you so — although I know you are a grown man in full faculty of his life. Mama worries as well and asks that I send you salutation. She wishes you to return, as do I.

As I opened the envelope, three round stones of the most intense black fell into my hand. Their beauty is otherworldly; anything else we own pales in comparison. I confess I clutched them in my hand, briefly debating keeping them to myself. For a moment holding those pearls, I was holding your hand, dear brother, and felt an absurd fear that they too might need to be sold as once were the bulk of our family valuables. Thankfully, sanity returned and I showed them to Mama. She was quite impressed with your gift as well.

Oh, Tobias! You do so love to scare me with your tales! Reading your account of climbing through those darkened caves and tunnels, I felt my own vision grown dark and the very breath seize in my chest. I very rarely have a fit of vapors; you know I am not as delicate as Mama. I want to hear every adventure, no matter how terrifying or beautiful. Just do be careful. You mention a new "adoptive" family and I fear that you are becoming so immersed in this foreign land that you are losing yourself. We are your family, waiting for you these many years in Savannah. Please come home to us in one piece.

The Tahitian dishes you describe seem quite exotic and I think I should like to taste them, if I am ever afforded the opportunity. I shudder to think what it would do to Mama's digestion. Speaking of delicious food, Thanksgiving will be here soon. I'll cook alongside Sarah, our remaining domestic servant. There will be, of course, turkey and stuffing, a hock of ham, gingerbread, pickles, apples and cheese, and mince pie. The only thing that will be missing is you.

I cannot be too melancholy, for truly you seem to be living in paradise. Meanwhile, autumn has arrived here again and another year's cycle is ending. Does time pass as swiftly out there on the island, surrounded by diamond and turquoise waters? Savannah is growing quickly, casting off the last remnants of a terrible war in time for a new century. As a symbol of this progress, a shiny new contraption traverses her streets. It's a new type of streetcar and runs along the Belt Line. Not powered by horse, mule or steam, but Electricity! Fancy that. They are quicker, cleaner and quieter. What is not to love?

Of course, Mama hates it. She says the railcar is just more propaganda and corruption from our oppressors to the North. (And how she goes on about the growing population of new residents, mostly Yankees.) I told her I was going to the market and then made a detour to Main Street, standing among the crowd to see the streetcar's inaugural run. I even rode it – the rides were free all day. I thought: 'If only Tobias were here to ride alongside me.' I know how much you fancy the new and curious.

In closing, sweet Tobias, I want to share a secret with you. I have kept it close to my heart, guarding it as jealously as the black pearls. I dare not tell another soul, especially Mama. But I know I can trust you with my fears and dreams and secrets. Here it is: I have fallen in love. He is a younger gentleman with a friendly, pleasant mien. His name is Dr. Samuels and he is a physician, newly moved to Savannah this past year and having set up a shingle downtown. I would pass him out and about in town almost every day, as if fate were conspiring towards us. I would see him at the market or the general store, and glance over just in time to see him glance away. It was quite endearing, his shy admiration.

It wasn't until six months had passed that we finally exchanged our first words. I was leaving the apothecary, having purchased medicines for Mama, when I suddenly lost my balance. I had stepped into one of those large ruts in the road, left by a horse streetcar no doubt. I fell quickly and quite inelegantly, sprawled in the dirt road. I lay stunned for a moment and had completely forgotten the bustle of the downtown street. Only the hard clip-clop of nearing hoof-beats followed by a shout brought my head up in time to see a large pair of geldings almost upon me.

Strong arms pulled me out of the way and there was Dr. Samuels, standing beside me. I'm not sure which of us was more surprised. I do believe he saved my life. My hat had flown off and my hair probably looked a fright, tumbled wildly about my face. My dress was ripped and dirty, but worst of all was the pain in my ankle. Such a wretched searing agony! I could not stand properly, let alone walk, in my heels and the weight of my clothes.

Dr. Samuels hailed a horse car and then picked me up — as if I weighed no more than a little girl! — and promptly took me to his office to examine the injury. You'll be pleased to know it was not broken, merely a severe sprain. He wouldn't take payment for his services and was so caring and solicitous that I believe I fell in love with him that very day.

Over a month has passed since that fateful afternoon and I have told no one — until now. He is a new transplant to Savannah, come from New York; one of the many Yankees invading our lovely city. Mama would hate him, life-saving hero that he is. I spend half my time berating my folly and the other half filled to bursting with the excitement of it all. I haven't felt such vigor since I met Robert. And it is because of that unhappy ending that I don't know if this can ever be more than a hidden pearl in my heart. I don't believe I can ever tell Mama and I live in fear that some gossip will reach her ears.

You have inspired me, Tobias. If you can go and crawl through pitch black caverns and jump off high cliffs in foreign lands, perhaps I can muster the courage to speak to Dr. Samuels when next we meet.

I remain your faithful sister,

Charlotte Rae

January 1, 1891

Dearest Charlotte Rae,

It brings my own spirit no end of goodness and light to know the heart of an independent-thinking woman still beats deep within my beloved sister. I realize you try to hide it beneath the fancy trappings of high-society life, cloaking it in the airs you put on for Mama and the other ladies of Savannah, but I know the true Charlotte Rae Beaumont. The Charlotte who would lose herself in love with a New York doctor and care little for gossiping whispers and Mama's protestations.

It is a new year, dear Charlotte. It is time to live for today, forget tomorrow. We are not so young as to afford many more regrets, our time under creation growing shorter every day. I already regret so much; I regret ever letting Louisa go, not fighting harder for her. I regret staying in Savannah too long. I regret standing by silently as Mama slowly drove Robert away from you. But I do not regret leaving Charleston for the war, as I would never have known Louisa otherwise, and my fond memories of her outweigh my regrets. I also would have missed the opportunity to befriend Robert on my way home from that God-forsaken prison camp. He proved a good and loyal compatriot and brought many a smile to your beautiful face. Your happiness could never be the source of regret. Whether you see him openly or keep your meetings discreet, if this Dr. Samuels makes you happy, do not let him slip away.

Electric trolley cars in Savannah—what will they think of next? I would have liked to join you on that ride. It sounds exciting. Steamships are the most new-fangled machines to be seen on these islands, but I'm not overly fond of them. They lack the history and majesty of sailing vessels. There is something to be said for the simplicity of life away from civilization. It is quieter, slower, and allows a man peace to gather his thoughts. This rain I could do without, though. It is rainy season, and there are months to go yet. It is not cold, in fact it is usually quite sultry, but it feels as though one spends five months straight constantly soaked to the bone. No matter; my hut is cool and dry most nights, and the company of my adoptive village is friendly and warm.

'Upa 'upa (The Firedance)

So that you might not feel alone in secrets you feel compelled to keep from Mama, I have one of my own to share with you. If you think your affections for a Yankee doctor would send her into a conniption, imagine her reaction to news of her only son losing his heart to a Tahitian woman. I first saw her this July past, at the open market in Papeete, the very day I sent my last letter. I noticed her across the square, hair as black as night, dark-skinned, tall, and fair of face, and my only thought became, 'I must look into her eyes.' It seems an odd thought, I know, but it became an obsession, to engage her in conversation so I could gaze into her eyes. However, this is not a simple task, for a foreign man to converse with a native woman. Arrangements needed to be made between my adoptive family and her family, and requirements met to prove my sincerity and worth. All this before they would even inquire as to her interest in meeting me! Not to mention the French looking down their noses at such a pairing, and the British missionaries all but forbidding it. Luckily, living far from Papeete spares me the sideways glances and whisperings.

Just as luckily, the trials I endured and passed to become a member of my village weighed heavily on the decisions, and once again, my scar and status as a former soldier proved a benefit. We were allowed to meet at a village feast this past November. So far, all of our visits together have been chaperoned, but I am confident that trust is building between her family and me and I remain patient in this courtship.

Her name is Matahina Taupua. I took one look into those deep, brown eyes I had longed to see, and was lost. It was as if I could see into her soul, and it proved more beautiful even than her flawless person. She is as if carved by Michelangelo in her physical perfection. Not once did she turn away from me; she even ran her fingers down the length of my scar, from temple to chin, and smiled. She had been told I am '*toanui*,' a mighty warrior from America, and she sought to meet me as much as I did her. She calls me *Tahitoa*, which means 'the first warrior,' because I'm the first American she's ever met. Her name means 'goddess eyes.' It could not be more appropriate.

So you see, Charlotte, I have thrown off my reservations and embraced life and love without fear of regret. You can do the same, I know it. I love Mama dearly, I truly do, but when will she ever allow us to live our lives as we see fit, if we do not simply take it? That is what I have done, I only hope and dream that you may find the strength in your fondness for this new man to do the same. I love you, Charlotte, and wish only happiness for you.

Until I see you again, I remain faithfully your loving brother,

Tobias

'UPA 'UPA (THE FIREDANCE)

June 6, 1891

Dear Brother,

I received your letter three weeks past. I read it immediately, as always impatient to hear news from you. I read it many times before storing it away in my desk, as I could not find the words to respond until today.

The hot, humid air of summer blankets Savannah and so much has happened since last we spoke. As you know, Mama has been unwell for some years now. Last winter, her symptoms worsened; her movements are not easy and she is more frequently tired. Mama's declining health gave me a reason to speak with Dr. Jacob Samuels. He has been most kind in prescribing medicinals easily obtained at the apothecary, though he still won't accept any payment.

On my second visit to his office, he asked to walk with me in the park. All the time I was afraid someone I knew would see us. Even more, I feared for my overall fate — the last time I had felt so was with Robert and that ended in one of the darkest times of my life. I also wondered what a handsome young doctor could want with a woman a score of years older. Still, when he asked to see me again, I answered with all my heart, 'yes'.

That was the beginning of our twice-weekly walks and I can't remember when last I felt such eager happiness. We continued to find common interests and passions — his favorite author is Jules Verne as well! I can hear your voice now: 'Fellow can't be that bad if he reads Verne.' He also supports women's suffrage, a cause close to my own heart. Mama, of course, does not, so I have always kept my views to myself. With Jacob, I do not feel the need to inhibit myself.

As winter faded and spring came into bloom, I met Jacob many more times. We enjoyed walks, going to the ice-cream parlor and even an evening at the theater. All the while, I hid my new relationship from Mama and if someone gave her word, she never said. Finally, the day came that Jacob asked for my hand in marriage. I was so very surprised, though I shouldn't have been, and happier than words can express. He wished to ask for your blessing but since you are not available, he requested to talk to Mama. You can imagine how my euphoria turned to horror.

I knew I must break the news to her gently; I remembered her frightful rage and then her silence for months after Robert and I married. I chose a quiet afternoon when Mama was sitting in the parlor. What happened next I struggle to find the words to tell you. Mama has suffered an apoplexy. She listened to my news; her brow creased and then she opened her mouth as if to respond… before keeling over. She lay on the floor as if dying and no amount of shaking or loud speech would rouse her.

I have no words for the terror I felt then, such as I had felt upon learning your capture by the Union army years ago. Calm your own dread Tobias, our mother is alive, thanks in great part to Jacob. I sent for him immediately and while his office is closer than Dr. Martin, I realize now it was that I trusted Jacob to save Mama's life.

Jacob arrived quickly with his black bag and physician's assistant. He moved Mama to the couch and performed a swift examination, diagnosing the apoplexy. Explaining that a prone position could 'exacerbate any cerebral haemorrhage,' he adjusted Mama to sit upright. I thought it strange to have an unconscious body positioned so, but I would have done anything. They started immediate treatment of ice to the head, a hot mustard footbath and a medicine Jacob called a 'rapidly acting cathartic.' Thankfully, he saw no need to use the leeches old Dr. Martin is so fond of.

Jacob cared for Mama thoroughly and intently; rolling up his shirtsleeves and transforming before my eyes from a quiet young man to a confident, educated physician capable of protecting his patients from the Grim Reaper himself. I had not yet seen this side of him and that day any remaining doubts about his proposal were laid to rest.

Shortly before dawn, Mama opened her eyes and spoke. My relief was short-lived as she seemed very weak and confused (as you well know, neither is her true nature). She believed that Jacob was her departed husband and that she was recovering on the childbirth bed. She continued to ask for her baby Tobias, at other times her darling boy Rufus, becoming increasingly agitated until Jacob gave her some laudanum to sleep.

Jacob assured me that her addled mind is a common side-effect of her infirmity. Mama needs to rest and be at ease, which has always been difficult for her disposition. Her recovery has been slow and at times it seems our mother will never be the same woman. I'm not sure if she recalls our conversation before she became ill and I do not know when it will be appropriate to broach, if ever. Jacob visits frequently now and Mama brightens to see him, though she still at times believes him to be our father, Rufus, or even you yourself. I fail to see any resemblance. I wonder if she would be so pleased to see him if she knew he was to be her new son-in-law.

Now I must respond to the events in your letter, another reason why I find myself at a loss for words. You have never heeded well the counsel of others, even when their wisdom could have saved you unnecessary hardship. Perhaps kept you from fighting in a brutal war that you were far too young to experience. You are a wilful man who forges his own path, undeterred by outside influence. Regardless, I beg you to listen this one time. I know you believe you have found love with this native woman, but you will not be able to bring her home and live in legal matrimony. The peace and harmony of married life and children will not be possible. Please, my dear brother, understand that I write this with the deepest love and respect for you. I have felt the consuming fire of forbidden love more than once in my lifetime. It is a hard enough path to travel when you come from different states. I fear your pursuit of a dark-skinned native will only bring heartache at home. Please brother, you do plan to come home?

I pray every night for your safe return as I pray for our mother's return to health.

Love always,

Charlotte Rae

4 December, 1891

My Dearest Charlotte Rae,

Without even reading past the greeting of your last letter, I knew you are cross with me. Although it does pain me to hear of Mama's infirmity, it pains me more to know your happiness still seems to be contingent upon her approval, no matter her state of mind. What shall you do, should she be revived from her feeblemindedness and return to her old self? I apologize for writing such harsh things, but I've seen your hopes raised this way in the past, only to be dashed by Mama's efforts to possess us.

This Dr Samuels does sound like a fine young man, indeed. I think you need not be so concerned with your 'advanced age' as you call it. A man who reads Verne certainly can't be too concerned with such trivialities, can he? I do hope you will allow yourself to be happy with him, despite your misgivings. It is no sin to pursue happiness, Charlotte, which leads me to my retort, dear sister.

It befuddles me to learn you support the sort of new thinking that will move us all forward into the coming new century, yet still hold on to tired old notions of a person's worth. You believe in woman's suffrage, yet insist I am wrong in my devotion to a woman who you obviously believe to be of low merit, without ever having met her. I know you will reply that it is not you, but polite society that dictates the cautions you are presenting me, but know that all the world is not Savannah. Or Tahiti, for that matter.

As I assure you, I do plan on coming home. I do not necessarily mean Georgia, but I do mean the United States. I hope to build a home for Matahina and myself in San Francisco, or possibly Seattle. I also hope to bring you to us in time, and now, your new doctor husband as well, assuming he is such at the time in which I send for you. And Mama, I suppose, if that is what it takes to get you there. But that is a bridge to cross at the proper time, and I hope with time's passage you might have a change of heart. So, enough of this discussion. Please do not remain cross with me. I have so much news for you.

It is my fondest hope, as always and despite your cross words, that this correspondence shall find you enjoying both good health and

'Upa 'upa (The Firedance)

high spirits. I am able to boast upon both. Tahiti's jungles, her inner sanctums, still offer me an idyllic paradise. One far from the colonial trappings of Papeete and the British missionaries bent on strangling the life from her. The lush greens of her foliage, the crystal-blue waters, the sounds of life surrounding me so completely; it is as if all the world were a celebration of the earthly senses. The birds that flitter about everywhere sport bright reds, blues and yellows, like party streamers. In all my years, I've never seen such a display of divine beauty.

A Frenchman, the painter Gauguin, has befriended me, though I suspect his kinship is motivated more by my secret cache of absinthe than by sincere camaraderie. Nonetheless, as I am merely a purveyor of words, lacking a single artistic bone in my body, he has honored me with the privilege of viewing some of his works before he sends them off to France. Every day he disappears into the jungle to paint, and at night he visits to drink my liquor and gossip before he returns to the hut he shares with his young Tahitian bride. I can't help but wonder if his wife in Paris knows of this arrangement.

The painting I found most striking is one that he calls 'The Fire Dance,' or 'Upa 'upa in the native Tahitian language. It is chaotic with color yet ordered in form; a great orange flame illuminating the jungle night, surrounded by dancers and seated onlookers. It captures every nuance of the natural beauty I mentioned earlier. I asked him if it came from his imagination or his witness. At first, he became tight-lipped, but after several hours and nearly a full bottle of my liquor, he let me in on a secret: despite the best efforts of the London Missionary Society to drive the native rituals and dances from the islands, they still take place deep in the jungles. Once he received the blessing of his bride's families, he became accepted as one of them, allowed to attend under vow of silence.

I asked him how he had achieved this acceptance. He said it was simple. He asked her to live with him. She said yes, but her mother insisted they live with an adoptive family for one month. If his beloved were still happy with him at the end of that time, they would be allowed to wed.

This sealed my resolve, dear sister, to commit to my love for Matahina. Before I could even dream of making her part of my world, of our world, dear sister, I needed to become part of her world in order to be accepted into it, in order to have her. I resolved to see this fire dance in person. In this quest, however, I fear I may have gone in over my head.

The Tahitians have become accustomed to Europeans, especially those they perceive as soft, artistic types, and Gauguin's trial was purposefully mild. My beloved's father, uncles and brothers are cut of warrior stock, and expect nothing less of me if they are to give me her hand. I had to go through their rite of passage.

I can think of no other word to describe it than 'roasting.' A great fire pit is built, a foot deep, eight feet long and three feet wide. It is burned overnight, constantly stoked until it is filled to the brim with hot coals. The following morning, the candidate is brought to the ritual site and made to lie down next to the pit. The drums and the dancing begin: slow at first, then building into a chaotic frenzy until they roll him right onto the coals!

I know I suffered much during the war, and I am no stranger to pain and fear it not, but that was nearly thirty years ago and I am not such a young man anymore. But whereas Louisa rejected me all those years ago because of what I endured, Matahina and her people embrace it. I watched as a boy, not much older than I when I first became a soldier, go through the ritual and come out recognized as a man, so I resolved to go through with it when my name was called.

Following the example set by the young man before me, I found myself writhing and convulsing and crying as if caught in the throws of a fit, my flesh smoking for a full five minutes or more, though it felt an eternity! Surprisingly, once released, the burns were quite mild. Apparently, the key to survival is in the shaking. To my horrific surprise, the coals were stoked again to be even hotter, and I was ordered to repeat the ritual! After the second round, the women were then called in to apply healing balms, but the amount of pain I endured cannot be denied. Despite this, my beloved's family now calls me warrior and kin.

We are to be married, in the traditional way of Matahina's people, on the eve of the New Year. The celebration will include the ritual dance 'upa 'upa, the firedance, as it is actually a celebration of fertility. However, it must be done in secret, on nearby Rangiroa, as the London Missionary Society, with the support of the French magistrate, has

‘Upa ’upa (The Firedance)

banned it and most traditional Tahitian dances. I know your misgivings for my decisions are now stronger than ever upon this revelation, but you know how well I do with silly rules and excessive authority, don't you, dear sister.

Please do not worry for me, Charlotte. I will be fine; I always survive to carry on. By the time you receive this, I will be happily married, as I hope you will be, too. Though I regret we will be worlds apart for both of our happiest days, it does not dampen my hopes for bright and joyous futures for both of us, together with our betrothed. And please don't burden Mama with any of this, especially if she is still in the infirm state you describe. As has been my usual practice, a second letter that is safe for reading aloud to her is included. Until I can look upon your shining, happy face again,

I remain your loyal brother,

Tobias

March 18, 1892

Dear Tobias,

I write to you with a heavy heart. The same week we received your letter, Mama passed away. I did not read your letter to her as we are both in agreement your adventures would have burdened her frail mind. It was a surprise she made the winter, but to lose her just as spring was blooming seems especially cruel.

Samuel took care of all the funeral arrangements. He was quite thorough and there was a reasonably large crowd. Mama did enjoy the society life. Of course, her oldest and dearest friends, Miss Susannah and Miss Becky, were in attendance, as well as a whole host of familiar faces, too many to name. Old parson Tomlin led the service and the house was filled with a silence broken only by some sobbing and the scraping of chairs. I could not shake the eerie sensation that mother was standing over my shoulder, as if watching the whole event. In her casket, she looked relaxed, as if merely slumbering. Perhaps she has found the peace she did not have in life. She is with our Lord Jesus now… and Papa and Rufus.

I was relieved when the three-day wake ended, and grateful that the weather had yet to warm much. The house was filled with flowers and candles, as you can imagine, yet it did nothing to dispel the pall of death. With the curtains all drawn, the mirrors covered in dark veils and the clocks all stopped, our modest home felt macabre and suffocating. I knew I could not live in our small townhouse any longer. Mama has gone to a better place and it is time I move on as well.

Samuel wishes us to be married this coming Sunday and I see no reason to delay further. How that man has found the patience to wait for me this long still astounds me. We are to move immediately into a home he purchased in the heart of downtown Savannah, near his practice. Samuel has agreed to let me help in his office; he understands that I need to be industrious and pursue interests away from the home. I feel I am the luckiest woman alive when I think of him. I look forward to Sunday as if it were every Christmas and birthday rolled into one. The only thing missing will be you. I wish with all my soul that you could give me away in the church.

'Upa 'upa (The Firedance)

If you were here with us, I would know you were safe. I worry something awful for you — you stop my poor heart from beating with your descriptions of Tahiti, her natives and their antics. This 'Fire Dance' sounds positively dreadful and disastrous. How could the fire not have burned you poor men alive? Are you truly unharmed? The ordeal sounds simply horrifying! When I read your description of going through the flames, I swear I smelled smoke. I felt a burning and tingling on my own skin! The whole ritual sounds barbaric, even for such primitive people. I beg you never to do it again, for my sake if not your own.

As for your new companion, the French painter seems a drunkard at best and bent on self-demise at worst. I can hear your chuckle now; I know I sound like Mama. I understand now her pain and fear, having lost almost everyone. I can't bear the thought of losing you Tobias, my only blood kin left in the world.

Brother, you know how much I love you and so hold your happiness in highest regard. I am glad you have found acceptance, however unconventional, and the love of a good woman. I can only assume she is good because you love her as well.

I simply cannot believe we will both be married and yet neither of us has met the other's betrothed. Never in all my imaginings did I think we would be so far apart, both orphans in the world. Please come home. Bring your new bride; we will make everything to rights. If not here in Savannah, then perhaps Atlanta? I hear they are much more forward-thinking there.

I feel my life on the cusp of something bright and new, almost complete except for you. Please leave that land of hard liquor and fire-walking and come home to us.

Awaiting your return—

All my love,

Charlotte Rae

9 January, 1892

My Dearest Charlotte Rae,

I write again so soon out of necessity. It is my hope this letter actually finds its way to you, as I must rely on my beloved's younger brother to ensure it reaches the mail ship from the United States. My news is both happy and yet not so good.

I am a married man now, but also a man with a price upon his life. Our wedding ceremony, magical; Matahina the most beautiful bride in all of time (only to be rivaled by you, dear sister, should you agree to wed your Dr Jacobs). The celebration following is the point at which events went awry.

It seems the London Missionary Society received word of our secret gathering on Rangiroa. Rumor has it Gauguin, in an effort to maintain his high status despite his own violations of the Society's bans, is the culprit. I fear I trusted too easily. A representative of the Society, along with a small contingent of French authorities, surprised our group in the midst of the fire dance. Mayhem ensued, of course. Although they were armed, we outnumbered them by far and they acquiesced in short order upon the contingency we promise to disband and allow them safe return to Papeete. However, this did not occur before one of the Frenchmen had treated Matahina in a manner entirely too rough for my sensibilities.

I lost my temper, Charlotte, and I fear vigorous island living has restored the strength I possessed in my youth, possibly even more so. I'd not raised a hand against another soul since the war; I did not think I could hit a man so hard as to end his life. Word is he lingered on in hospital for a week, only to expire day before last. In that moment, the 'odd American journalist', as I have come to be known, gained new infamy as a fugitive from the French and British Authorities.

Fear not, Charlotte. Their influence does not extend past the Islands of Tahiti, and I have acquired passage, in secret, back to the U.S. mainland. Seattle, specifically. As fate would have it, an old friend tracked me down in San Francisco, by my reportage in *The Morning Call*. He came all the way to Tahiti to find me. Surely you remember Karl Blackmon, the big man, my close compatriot from my time with

Mosby's Rangers? He was a sea captain by trade before the war, and like me, found his way again in San Francisco. He commands his own ship once more, *Angelina's Fury*, and he arrived in Papeete on the same day as the Frenchman's death, landing to the news of my criminal accusations. Still the ever-resourceful scout, he found me by way of Matahina's family. It is aboard his fair vessel that I write this. We leave Rangiroa, where Matahina and I have been hiding, as soon as the ink of this letter has dried and Matahina's brother departs the ship with it.

Please do not worry for me, dearest Charlotte. I will send you word by telegram the very moment Matahina and I land in Seattle. And certainly do not burden Mama with this development. Carry on as you would, as if this letter never arrived, and let your young Dr Jacobs continue to make you a happy woman.

All my love, your faithful brother,

Tobias

The Western Union Telegraph Company

Dated April 1, 1892

Received at 66 College Lane

To Miss Charlotte Rae Beaumont

Angelina's Fury found abandoned at sea stop
En route Hawaii to Seattle stop No survivors
found stop

Per direct instructions Tobias Beaumont stop
Your brother's accumulated earnings stop
Attached bank transfer $3287 to Charlotte
Beaumont stop One final instruction stop Don't
tell Mama stop

My condolences for your loss stop Ronald Matthew
Simpson, Editor, The Morning Call stop

ABOUT THE CONTRIBUTORS

GARY BONN lives in Scotland, with his family and an alarming number of accident-prone chickens. His writing is informed by his long experience working with children with social, behavioural or mental health difficulties and equally by his fascination with hunter-gatherer societies. He throws a mean spear. His novels, *Expect Civilian Casualties* and *The Evil And The Fear* are published by Firedance Books.

* * * *

JANET ALLISON BROWN is the author of dozens of children's picture books and editor of several volumes of academic papers. She has written explorer guides, restaurant reviews, and articles on a range of subjects including traditional Arabic ship-building and handicrafts, adoption, education, faith and ancient cave paintings. Wife, mother, home-educator, writer and editor, she was educated at Balliol College, Oxford, and lives in rural Derbyshire. She likes stories, and makes them up all the time. Her novel, *The Walker's Daughter*, is published by Firedance Books.

* * * *

LOUISE COLE is older than she behaves but younger than she looks. Over-educated and totally lacking in financial ambition, she has nevertheless managed to hold down various jobs in journalism and publishing. She finally forsook the lure of a regular paycheck to run her own media agency in North Yorkshire, thinking that quality time with her family and her writing would more than compensate for the lack of money. Yeah, well, you have to try these things. Louise contributes shorts to Writerlot.

* * * *

JAE ERWIN Stepping away from the world of occupational psychology and small business consultancy, Jae rackets around between writing, teaching yoga and exploring anything weird and wonderful that takes her fancy. She lives on the Pennines, has a husband, three sons, a dog, two cats and four vegetable beds – don't ask her which one she loves the most. Her novel, *Stillness Dancing*, is published by Firedance Books.

* * * *

ALISON GARDINER writes YA novels, picture books, non-fiction, women's fiction, film scripts: a polygenre. Four children keep her in touch with her readers and technology, and out of touch with her bank balance and any chance of a calm, sensible life. For which she is grateful. Loving travelling, fantasy, mystery and laughter means there is a constant swirl of stories inside her head and it's a brilliant feeling to let them flow out. Broadcasting weekly on Radio Litopia gives her the chance to chat to many authors, which keeps her dreaming. Life is too short to be serious.

* * * *

STEPHEN GODDEN writes speculative fiction. He reads pretty much anything. He uses the second to fuel the first. (And writes this stuff in the third, because somebody told him once that he should and he didn't like to argue.) Other than that, Steve's just a bloke of independent penury and incidental personality. He also writes under the name T F Grant. Well, gotta have some variety in your life.

* * * *

ALF HAYWOOD A salesman for most of his adult life, Alf has decided to brush off retirement in favour of being a full-time writer (the fool). He started writing romance and adventure stories about three years ago. Now his mission is to prove to his wife and family that all those hours huddled over a computer in his office were not wasted.

* * * *

SHUNA MEADE and her husband sold everything they owned and left the UK in 2004 bound for a tropical island in the Caribbean. Paradise inspires her to write fiction and poetry. Her non-fiction pieces about the realities of island life can be found on www.writerlot.net under the pseudonym Island Writer. She has had numerous short stories published in anthologies and has an adult novel and YA novel in progress. Shuna is a graduate of St Andrew's University in Scotland where she studied English and History and has been a writer in hiding for as long as she can remember.

* * * *

LILLIAN REYES was born and raised in Norfolk, Virginia. She has spent the last couple years traveling the globe and serving in the US Peace Corps. She has a BA in Environmental Studies and Political Science from Virginia Wesleyan College. Her previous publications have been non-fiction, including articles for *Green Careers Journal* and *Fourth Day Universe*. Lillian's earliest memories are of being surrounded by books and playing at the library; she believes stories are a mirror of their contemporary society as well as gateways to other worlds.

* * * *

BILL SAUER is a former musician, former photographer, graphic designer by day, and writer by night and weekend. He has scribbled down millions of words since childhood. The words just come, and who are we to try and stop them? Husband, brother to a legion of siblings, doggie daddy to mutts and strays. Often mistaken for a big, dumb gorilla until proven otherwise, which is how Bill likes it. Then it's always a pleasant surprise when the truth is discovered: that boy can write, can't he? Especially when it's Bill doing the discovering.

* * * *

REN WAROM is a writer of speculative oddities, not known for an ability to fit into boxes of any description. She's a certified Pirate-nun, mum to three spawn, slave to several cats, writing obsessive and general weirdo. The word askance was invented for the way people tend to look at her. For her sins, Ren is now represented by the fabulous Jennifer Udden of the Donald Maass Literary Agency. At some point, evidence of this union will land in a bookshop near you. It's recommended you buy hazard gear in preparation.

ALSO AVAILABLE!

Available from Firedance Books...

OUT OF NOWHERE by Patrick LeClerc

An urban fantasy, pacy, funny and compelling to the last page...

Healer Sean Danet is immortal—a fact he has cloaked for centuries, behind army lines and now a paramedic's uniform. Having forgotten most of his distant past, he has finally found peace—and love.

But there are some things you cannot escape, however much distance you put behind you. When Sean heals the wrong man, he uncovers a lethal enemy who holds all the cards. And this time he can't run.

It's time to stand and fight, for himself, for his friends, for the woman he loves. It's time, finally, for Sean to face his past—and choose a future.

A story of love, of battle—and of facing your true self when there's nowhere left to hide.

Available from Firedance Books...

THE WALKER'S DAUGHTER by Janet Allison Brown

When her mother dies at the hands of a silver-haired figure in black, six-year-old spirit-walker Cora Bloux hides out in her own body. Twenty years later she's still there, fiercely maintaining an outwardly stable, conventional life.

But when her own daughter is hit by a car, Cora is forced to spirit-walk again—and discovers that the spirit world has been waiting for her.

In the extraordinary, fast-paced world of spirit-walkers, body-swappers, rock bands and second chances, Cora must discover her true self and learn the ordinary lessons of courage, trust and love.

To see the world as it really is, sometimes you have to close your eyes and... walk.

ALSO AVAILABLE!

Available from Firedance Books...

THE EVIL AND THE FEAR by Gary Bonn

An ancient magic released. A world of pain and fear hurtling towards catastrophe. A collision that will bring death and destruction to mankind.

Only two young women stand between the fury of the magic and the apathy of the world. Unfortunately one of them is dead and the other one is psychotic.

While her dead friend holds the fury of the magic at bay, Beatha must journey into the half-world to discover the secret at the heart of all things...

But a journey like this requires allies and, in Beatha's case, a truck-load of medication. Is the world ready for heroes like these?

The Evil And The Fear is a wildly inspirational story about being more than people expect, and learning to expect more than you ever believed was possible.

Available from Firedance Books...

TALES OF THE SHONRI: CITY OF LIGHTS by Stephen Godden

Darkness never falls in the City of Lights. The last hope of a broken world, the remaining Shonri warriors brave the ever-vigilant city to fight their war against the vicious Magi—or meet their deaths. For the last witch Medina, powerful, seductive, and untrustworthy, has sold her art to their enemies.

Can the handful of Shonri end the battle before Medina's magic reveals them? Can Medina survive her attempts to use the Magi for her own means? And can any of them live with the results of the battle they are about to face...

For while they scheme and fight, something stirs beneath the City of Lights... something more perilous than death itself...

ALSO AVAILABLE!

Available from Firedance Books...

EXPECT CIVILIAN CASUALTIES by Gary Bonn

Jason has spent the last six years living wild on beaches. Now he's seventeen and a feral girl walks into his life.

A girl with no name.

He calls her Anna. She's fun, she's kind — and she's the most dangerous person in the world.

The most unusual love story, and a truly strange war story... Expect Civilian Casualties turns how we see the world upside down.

Available from Firedance Books...

BROKEN WORLDS Volume One

What do we do when God becomes an unwanted houseguest, you're in love with the wrong girl and aliens decide to eat California? Take a wild ride with 15 writers from around the globe to discover their version of a broken world... and the humour, compassion and love which saves us. From murder to manga, heartbreak to horror, *Broken Worlds* dances us through times, genres and worlds. Prepare to be thrilled, tickled, scared and enchanted... it's one hell of a ride.

Available from Firedance Books...

THE BEST OF WRITERLOT Volume One

Wild women, warriors, the first moments of love. Muses, metafiction and murder. Find new voices, new series and cracking stories in this dizzying collection from the WriterLot team. WriterLot.net produces great new fiction for its followers every day. This collection celebrates some of the best, filled with unforgettable characters, heart-stopping action, and the trembling uncertainty of personal relationships. It captures the essence of what it is to be human (or, in one case, what it is to be a dog).

www.ingramcontent.com/pod-product-compliance
Lightning Source LLC
Chambersburg PA
CBHW060813120626
46557CB00001B/203

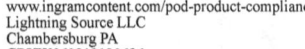